# A Few Good Men

## by Aaron Sorkin

A SAMUEL FRENCH ACTING EDITION

FOUNDED 1830

NEW YORK HOLLYWOOD LONDON TORONTO

SAMUELFRENCH.COM

**ISBN 978-0-573-70051-4**     Printed in U.S.A.     #8146

## MUSIC USE NOTE

Licensees are solely responsible for obtaining formal written permission from copyright owners to use copyrighted music in the performance of this play and are strongly cautioned to do so. If no such permission is obtained by the licensee, then the licensee must use only original music that the licensee owns and controls. Licensees are solely responsible and liable for all music clearances and shall indemnify the copyright owners of the play and their licensing agent, Samuel French, Inc., against any costs, expenses, losses and liabilities arising from the use of music by licensees.

The various military chants included in *A FEW GOOD MEN*, whose use is both necessary and mandatory in productions, are under copyright protection. MUSIC ROYALTY IS AS FOLLOWS:

**Amateur Productions:** $2.50 per performance, all-inclusive.

**Stock Productions:** Terms quoted on application,

## IMPORTANT BILLING AND CREDIT
## REQUIREMENTS

All producers of *A FEW GOOD MEN* *must* give credit to the Author of the Play in all programs distributed in connection with performances of the Play, and in all instances in which the title of the Play appears for the purposes of advertising, publicizing or otherwise exploiting the Play and/or a production. The name of the Author *must* appear on a separate line on which no other name appears, immediately following the title and *must* appear in size of type not less than fifty percent of the size of the title type.

In addition the following credit *must* be given in all programs and publicity information distributed in association with this piece:

**Broadway production presented by David Brown, Lewis Allen,
Robert Whitehead, Roger L. Stevens, Kathy Levin,
Suntory International Corporation, and The Shubert Organization**

*A FEW GOOD MEN* was originally presented at the Heritage Repertory Theatre of the Univeristy of Virginia, Department of Drama, and subsequently, in association with the John F. Kennedy Center for the Performing Arts, was presented at the Music Box Theatre in New York, on November 15, 1989, under the direction of Don Scardino, with Dianne Trulock as production stage manager, and with designs by: Ben Edwards, set; David C. Woolard, costume; Thomas R. Skelton, light; and John Gromada, sound; and the cast was as follows:

**SENTRY** . . . . . . . . . . . . . . . . . . . . . . . . . . . . . . . . . . . . . . . . . . . . . . . Ron Ostrow

**HAROLD DAWSON** . . . . . . . . . . . . . . . . . . . . . . . . . . . . . . . . . . . . Victor Love

**LOUDEN DOWNEY** . . . . . . . . . . . . . . . . . . . . . . . . . . . . . . Michael Dolan

**SAM WEINBURG** . . . . . . . . . . . . . . . . . . . . . . . . . . . . . . . . . . . Mark Nelson

**DANIEL A. KAFFEE** . . . . . . . . . . . . . . . . . . . . . . . . . . . . . . . . . Tom Hulce

**JOANNE GALLOWAY** . . . . . . . . . . . . . . . . . . . . . . . . . . . Megan Gallagher

**ISAAC WHITAKER** . . . . . . . . . . . . . . . . . . . . . . . . . . . . . . . Edmond Genest

**MATTHEW A. MARKINSON** . . . . . . . . . . . . . . . . . . . . . . . . . Robert Hogan

**WILLIAM T. SANTIAGO** . . . . . . . . . . . . . . . . . . . . . . . . . . Arnold Molina

**NATHAN JESSEP** . . . . . . . . . . . . . . . . . . . . . . . . . . . . . . . . . Stephen Lang

**JONATHAN JAMES KENDRICK** . . . . . . . . . . . . . . . . . . . . . . . Ted Marcoux

**JACK ROSS** . . . . . . . . . . . . . . . . . . . . . . . . . . . . . . . . . . . . . . . Clark Gregg

**JEFFREY OWEN HOWARD** . . . . . . . . . . . . . . . . . . . . . . . . Geoffrey Nauffts

**JULIUS ALEXANDER RANDOLPH** . . . . . . . . . . . . . . . . . . . . . . Paul Butler

**WALTER STONE** . . . . . . . . . . . . . . . . . . . . . . . . . . . . . . . . . . Fritz Sperberg

**MARINES, SAILORS, M.P.'S, LAYWERS, et al.** . . . . Stephen Bradbury, Jeffrey Dreisbach

# CHARACTERS

LANCE CPL. HAROLD W. DAWSON
PFC LOUDEN DOWNEY
LT. J.G. SAM WEINBERG
LY. J.G. DANIEL A. KAFFEE
LT. CMDR. JOANNE GALLOWAY
CAPT. ISAAC WHITAKER
CAPT. MATTHEW A. MARKINSON
PFC. WILLIAM T. SANTIAGO
LT. COL. NATHAN JESSEP
LT. JONATHAN JAMES KENDRICK
LT. JACK ROSS
CPL. JEFFREY OWEN HOWARD
CAPT. JULIUS ALEXANDER RANDOLPH
CMDR. WALTER STONE
MARINES, SAILORS, M.P.'S, LAYWERS, et al.

# SCENE

The action takes place in various locations in Washington, D.C., and on the United States Naval Base in Guantanomo Bay, Cuba.

# TIME

Summer, 1986

**DAWSON.** I, Lance Corporal Harold W. Dawson, have been informed by Special Agent R.C. McGuire of the Naval Investigative Service, that I am suspected of Murder, Conspiracy to Commit Murder, and Conduct Unbecoming a United States Marine in the matter of Private First Class William T. Santiago. I have also been advised that I have the right to remain silent and make no statement at all.

**DOWNEY.** Any statement I do make can be used against me in a trial by court-martial or other judicial or administrative proceeding. I have the right to consult with a lawyer prior to further questioning.

**DAWSON.** I am presently assigned to Rifle Security Company Windward, Second Platoon Delta, NAVBASE, Guantanamo Bay, Cuba.

**DOWNEY.** I am a PFC in the United States Marine Corps assigned to Marine Rifle Security Company Windward, Second Platoon Delta. I will have been in the Marine Corps ten months as of August.

**DAWSON.** I entered Private Santiago's barracks room on the evening of 6 July, at or about 23:50. I was accompanied by PFC Louden Downey.

**DOWNEY.** I was accompanied by my squad leader, Lance Corporal Harold W. Dawson.

**DAWSON.** We tied his hands and feet with rope.

**DOWNEY.** We tied Private Santiago's hands and feet with rope and we forced a piece of cloth into his mouth.

**DAWSON.** We placed duct tape over his eyes and mouth.

**DOWNEY.** I have read this two page statement that Special Agent McGuire has prepared for me at my request, as we discussed its content. I have been allowed to make all changes and corrections, initializing those changes and corrections.

**DAWSON.** These statements are true and factual to the best of my knowledge.

(*Lights up on* **KAFFEE**'s *office.*)

(**SAM** *is entering.* **KAFFEE**'s *in a hurry.*)

**SAM.** Danny –

**KAFFEE.** I'm late.

**SAM.** You know what I just saw?

**KAFFEE.** No, but I'm genuinely late.

**SAM.** There's a lady lawyer from internal affairs wandering around the hallway.

**KAFFEE.** What's she doing?

**SAM.** I don't know.

**KAFFEE.** Is she stealing things?

**SAM.** No.

**KAFFEE.** Tell me why I care.

**SAM.** Ordinarily, when internal affairs sends a lawyer around to talk to the lawyers, it means someone's screwed up.

**KAFFEE.** Do you think it's you?

**SAM.** No.

**KAFFEE.** Have you done anything wrong?

**SAM.** No.

**KAFFEE.** You sure?

**SAM.** Yes I'm sure. I think so. I don't know, I've been very tired lately. Look, do me a favor, would you?

**KAFFEE.** Sure.

**SAM.** If she talks to you, if she mentions anything about DeMattis –

**KAFFEE.** Who?

**SAM.** DeMattis. The engineer. Remember, my guy who was littering in the admiral's tulip garden. I may have cut a few corners. Would you cover me?

**KAFFEE.** Sure.

**SAM.** Yeah?

**KAFFEE.** I don't know what you're talking about, but sure, no problem.

**SAM.** DeMattis. He's an engineer –

**KAFFEE.** Littering in the Admiral's turnip garden.

**SAM.** Tulips.

**KAFFEE.** Okay.

**SAM.** Where are you going?

**KAFFEE.** I'm representing an ensign who bought and smoked ten dollars worth of oregano.

**SAM.** He thought it was weed?

**KAFFEE.** I can only hope.

**SAM.** You're not concerned?

**KAFFEE.** What's he gonna be charged with, possession of a condiment? He'll get a C Misdemeanor, 15 days restricted duty.

**SAM.** I'm talking about the lady from internal affairs, you're not concerned?

**KAFFEE.** My softball team's playing Bethesda Medical tomorrow, I can't be concerned with anything right now. I'll see you at lunch.

(**KAFFEE** *exits as* – )

(*Lights up on* **WHITAKER**'s *office.*)

**JO.** I'm Lt. Commander Joanne Galloway, sir.

**WHITAKER.** Captain Whitaker, come on in.

**JO.** I appreciate your seeing me on such short notice.

**WHITAKER.** Bronsky said you were reopening a case.

**JO.** Yes sir.

**WHITAKER.** Bronsky and I go way back.

**JO.** He speaks very highly of you, sir.

**WHITAKER.** Yeah, that's bullshit, right?

**JO.** Yes sir.

**WHITAKER.** I know you, don't I?

**JO.** I don't believe we've formally –

**WHITAKER.** You work at internal affairs.

**JO.** Yes sir.

**WHITAKER.** I hate internal affairs.

**JO.** Yes sir.

**WHITAKER.** And you're a woman.

**JO.** Yes sir.

**WHITAKER.** Well that's all right.

**JO.** Thank you, sir.

**WHITAKER.** You were the one who recycled those 14 B Misdemeanors last winter.

**JO.** That may have been me.

**WHITAKER.** 14 B Misdemeanors. Drunk and Disorderlies. We had 'em closed.

**JO.** No sir, you didn't. The blue copies of the charge sheets weren't filed to Division with the IC-1.

**WHITAKER.** *(pause)* Who gives a shit??!!

**JO.** My boss, the Judge Advocate General.

**WHITAKER.** He doesn't care any more than I do, it was *you.*

**JO.** There are rules, sir, I'm sure you understand.

**WHITAKER.** You had my guys working Christmas day, filling out charge sheets in long hand. Christmas day, Commander.

**JO.** It was in the interest of justice, sir.

**WHITAKER.** Okay, are you here to bother anybody?

**JO.** Absolutely not. No, sir. Not at all. Only if necessary.

**WHITAKER.** What can I do for you?

**JO.** Two prisoners are being held in Guantanamo Bay, Cuba. They pleaded guilty to Murder 2, Conspiracy to Commit, and Conduct Unbecoming. Over the weekend, I petitioned Captain Bronsky to deny the guilty pleas, and to order the prisoners moved here to Washington to be assigned council.

**WHITAKER.** What was the problem with the guilty pleas? Somebody mis-spell Conspiracy?

**JO.** No sir, but the prisoners confessed to murder at three o'clock in the morning during a twenty minute interview at which neither had an attorney.

**WHITAKER.** So Bronsky's bringing 'em up to Washington.

**JO.** You'll be receiving a memo from Division instructing you to assign an attorney from your department. Which brings me to why I'm here.

**WHITAKER.** Yes.

**JO.** I'd like a favor.

**WHITAKER.** Good luck to you.

**JO.** Thank you.

**WHITAKER.** What's the favor?

**JO.** Tell Division you want to assign a lawyer *outside* your department.

**WHITAKER.** Why?

**JO.** Because I'm a lawyer outside your department.

**WHITAKER.** And don't think I'm not grateful.

**JO.** I've brought a letter of recommendation from Captain Bronsky.

**WHITAKER.** You're an investigator, why do you want to get mixed up in grunt work.

**JO.** I don't consider it grunt work, sir.

**WHITAKER.** It's a five minute plea bargain and a week of paperwork.

**JO.** I'd look forward to it with relish, sir.

**WHITAKER.** And can I ask, do you always talk as if your dialogue was written by someone who's not very good at it?

**JO.** I'm sorry if my over-eagerness is grating.

**WHITAKER.** It's not, it's endearing. You could have a career as a cartoon squirrel.

**JO.** I want to make sure this is handled properly.

**WHITAKER.** Have you done litigation before?

**JO.** My first year with the JAG Corps.

**WHITAKER.** How many cases did you handle?

**JO.** Altogether?

**WHITAKER.** Yes.

**JO.** Six.

**WHITAKER.** How'd you do?

**JO.** From what perspective?

**WHITAKER.** Your client's.

**JO.** Not well.

**WHITAKER.** Okay.

(*A* **LAWYER** *enters with an inter-office memo and hands it to* **WHITAKER.**)

**LAWYER.** Excuse me, Isaac, this just came for you. It's from Division.

**JO.** Those cases were lost on their merits, sir.

**WHITAKER.** (*to the* **LAWYER**) This is Lt. Commander Joanne Galloway.

**LAWYER.** Really?

**JO.** How do you do?

**LAWYER.** Really enjoyed last Christmas.

**WHITAKER.** (*to the* **LAWYER**) That'll be all.

(*The* **LAWYER** *exits.* **WHITAKER** *is looking over the memo.*)

**JO.** So what do you say?

**WHITAKER.** Commander – may I call you Joanne?

**JO.** Yes. Please.

**WHITAKER.** Joanne, you seem like a fairly harmless neurotic person –

**JO.** I appreciate that.

**WHITAKER.** And I'd like to help you out, but there are two things preventing me. The first is that while I sincerely believe that in your present assignment with internal affairs you do an exceptionally thorough job, I have a hunch that as a litigator…you know, not so much.

**JO.** Yes, but –

**WHITAKER.** The second is that Division already chose an attorney.

(**JO**'s *a little shocked.*)

**JO.** (*pause*) What?

**WHITAKER.** *(showing her the memo)* They've already assigned someone. I'm not sure why they care, but it's out of my hands now. They want you to brief the man. Apparently you've got some letters and documents.

**JO.** Yes.

**WHITAKER.** We have a staff meeting at three, I'll be giving out assignments then. Come by, do your thing, try not to make anyone cry.

**JO.** Yes sir.

**WHITAKER.** Tough break.

**JO.** Thank you, Captain.

**WHITAKER.** You can call me Isaac.

**JO.** And what's the name of the attorney?

*(DAWSON and DOWNEY snap to attention in the brig.)*

**DAWSON.** Ten-hut. Officer on deck.

**WHITAKER.** Daniel Kaffee.

*(Lights up on brig.)*

*(MARKINSON enters. Quietly and with difficulty, he addresses DAWSON and DOWNEY)*

**MARKINSON.** They're giving you a lawyer. They're gonna move you up to Washington D.C. and give you a lawyer who's gonna ask you some questions. I want you to remember something about these lawyers. They don't care about anything. They don't care about honor or loyalty. They don't care about Colonel Jessep or Lt. Kendrick, they don't care about me and they don't care about you. They're clowns. That is why, so help me God, they're the only ones who can save you right now.

*(beat)*

I want you boys to be smart. Talk to your lawyer.

*(We hear WHITAKER speaking from the staff meeting.)*

**WHITAKER.** I'd just settle for the O.T.H., it's his fourth U.A., you're not gonna do any better than that.

*(Lights up on the staff meeting.)*

**LAWYER #1.** I don't think I need to settle for the O.T.H. if I file a motion to suppress, I can –

**WHITAKER.** A motion to suppress?

**LAWYER #1.** Absolutely.

**WHITAKER.** On what grounds?

**LAWYER #1.** *(pause)* Grounds?

**LAWYER #2.** See, this is where your strategy begins to fall apart.

**WHITAKER.** Take the O.T.H.

*(**KAFFEE** enters.)*

**KAFFEE.** Excuse me, I'm sorry I'm late.

**WHITAKER.** I'm sure you have a good excuse.

**KAFFEE.** No, I just didn't really care enough about this meeting to be on time.

**WHITAKER.** *(to **JO**)* He's kidding. Commander Galloway, this is Lt. Kaffee.

**KAFFEE.** How do you do?

**JO.** You're a J.G.

**KAFFEE.** I beg your pardon?

**JO.** *(to **WHITAKER**)* This is the attorney Division assigned?

**WHITAKER.** Yes.

**JO.** I wrote a seventeen page memo to Bronsky outlining the situation, I pleaded my case for a half hour in his living room on a Sunday afternoon, and Division assigned a Lt. Junior Grade?

**KAFFEE.** Have I come at a bad time?

**WHITAKER.** *(to **KAFFEE**)* Commander Galloway's from internal affairs.

**KAFFEE.** Oh. Ahhh…Whatever Sam did with the guy in the tulip garden, it wasn't his fault, he was tired. *(to **SAM**)* How's that?

**SAM.** Thanks very much.

**KAFFEE.** Sam has a baby at home and he's sure she's about to say her first word any day now.

**WHITAKER.** How do you know?

**SAM.** She just looks like she has something to say.

**WHITAKER.** She's fourteen months old, what could she have to say?

**KAFFEE.** We've got a pool going if you want to get in on it. Ten bucks. Pick a word off the grid.

**WHITAKER.** What's left?

**KAFFEE.** Rosebud.

**JO.** Captain, with all due respect –

**WHITAKER.** Let's get started. Danny, Commander Galloway's here 'cause you've been detailed by Division.

*("Oooh's" and "Ahhh's" from the other* **LAWYERS.***)*

**KAFFEE.** Detailed to do what?

**WHITAKER.** Detailed to handle this.

*(***WHITAKER*** hands him some files.)*

Everybody listen up: Guantanamo Bay, Cuba. A Marine PFC named William Santiago writes a letter claiming he knows the name of a Marine on the base who illegally fired a round from his weapon over the fenceline. Santiago ends the letter by saying he wants a transfer off the base in exchange for the identity of the Marine.

**KAFFEE.** What's a fenceline?

**WHITAKER.** Sam?

**SAM.** A big wall separating the good guys from the bad guys.

**KAFFEE.** Okay.

**WHITAKER.** The man who fired over the fenceline was Santiago's squad leader, Lance Corporal Harold Dawson. The fenceline shooting, however, is completely beside the point.

**KAFFEE.** What's the point?

**WHITAKER.** Santiago's dead.

**SAM.** What happened?

**WHITAKER.** Dawson and another member of the squad, PFC Louden Downey, went into Santiago's room, tied his hands and feet and stuck a rag into his mouth. The doctor said the rag must have been treated with some kind of toxin.

**KAFFEE.** They poisoned the rag?

**WHITAKER.** Not according to them.

**KAFFEE.** What do they say?

**WHITAKER.** Not much. They're being brought up here tomorrow morning. Thursday at oh-six-hundred you'll catch a transport down to Cuba for the day to find out what you can. Commander Galloway's gonna fill you in on the rest. Any questions so far?

**KAFFEE.** Was that oh-six-hundred in the morning, sir?

**WHITAKER.** Division wants me to assign back-up. Any volunteers?

**SAM.** No.

**WHITAKER.** Sam.

**SAM.** Sir, I have a pile of work on my desk that –

**WHITAKER.** Work with Kaffee on this.

**SAM.** Doing what?

**WHITAKER.** Various administrative...you know...things. Back up. Whatever.

**SAM.** In other words I have no responsibilities whatsoever.

**WHITAKER.** Right.

**SAM.** My kinda case.

**JO.** Lt. Kaffee, how long have you been in the Navy?

**KAFFEE.** I'm sorry?

**JO.** How long have you been in the Navy?

**KAFFEE.** Going on nine months now.

**JO.** Have you ever been in a courtroom?

**KAFFEE.** I once had my driver's license suspended.

**JO.** Alright. Captain this is absurd –

**WHITAKER.** Danny. Commander, if this thing ever went to court, those Marines wouldn't need a lawyer, they'd need a priest.

**JO.** No, they'd need a lawyer.

**KAFFEE.** Isaac, I'd like to say for the record that this is the least fun I've ever had at one of your staff meetings.

**WHITAKER.** *(to JO)* Lt. Kaffee's generally considered one of the best litigators in our office. He's successfully plea bargained 44 cases in less than a year.

**KAFFEE.** One more and I get a set of steak knives.

*(JO takes a large file out of her briefcase and hands it to SAM.)*

**JO.** One of the people you'll be talking to down there is the barracks C.O., Colonel Nathan Jessep, I assume you've heard of him.

**KAFFEE.** *(pause)* Sam?

**SAM.** He's been in the papers lately. He's expected to be appointed Director of Operations for the NSC. Golden boy of the Corps. Very big inside the DOD.

**KAFFEE.** How does somebody get very big inside the DOD? Is he touring, did he cut an album?

*(JO hands KAFFEE a stack of letters.)*

**JO.** On top is an inventory of Santiago's foot locker on the night he died. Four pairs of camouflage pants, three long sleeve khaki shirts, three short sleeve khaki shirts, three pairs of boots, four pairs of green socks, four pairs of black socks –

**KAFFEE.** Commander?

**JO.** Yes.

**KAFFEE.** I'm not sure that socks and underwear are gonna figure too heavily into this defense.

**JO.** I'm saying we need to get his personal belongings to his family after they've cleared evidence.

**KAFFEE.** Sam, you're in charge of socks and underwear.

**SAM.** So it's a good thing I went to school for 21 years.

**JO.** *(ignoring)* These are letters that Santiago wrote in his eight months at GITMO –

**SAM.** *(to KAFFEE)* Guantanamo Bay.

**KAFFEE.** I knew that one.

**JO.** He wrote to his recruiter, HQ Atlantic, the Commandant of the Marine Corps, even his senator. He wanted to be transferred off the base. Nobody was listening. You with me?

**KAFFEE.** Yes.

**JO.** Finally he wrote this letter –

(*She hands it to* **KAFFEE**, *who hands it to* **SAM**.)

– where he offered information about Corporal Dawson's fenceline shooting in exchange for a transfer. This letter is the only physical evidence establishing a motive for Dawson to kill Santiago.

**KAFFEE.** Gotcha.

(*beat*)

And Santiago is who?

**JO.** (*beat*) The victim.

**KAFFEE.** (*to* **SAM**) Write that down. (*to* **JO**) Am I right in assuming these letters don't paint a flattering picture of Santiago's treatment by the Marine Corps?

**JO.** Yes, among other–

**KAFFEE.** And am I also right in assuming that a protracted investigation of the incident might cause some embarrassment for Sinatra?

**JO.** Who?

**KAFFEE.** The Base Commander, the guy who's hot at the Pentagon.

**JO.** Colonel Jessep, yes, but the point –

**KAFFEE.** Twelve years.

**JO.** I'm sorry?

**KAFFEE.** I'll get it knocked down to Involuntary Manslaughter. Twelve years. They'll probably be home in seven.

**JO.** You haven't talked to a witness or looked at a piece of paper.

**KAFFEE.** Pretty impressive.

**JO.** Either that or criminally stupid. Which do you guess I'm thinking it is right now?

**WHITAKER.** Kids –

**KAFFEE.** Excuse me, sir. Ma'am, do you have some sort of jurisdiction here that I should know about?

**JO.** I'm special counsel for internal affairs, Lieutenant, my jurisdiction's pretty much in your face. Read the letters. *(to WHITAKER)* Thank you for the time, Captain.

**WHITAKER.** You're not leaving already, are you?

**JO.** Yes sir. I need to audit the paper work on an engineer who was found littering in the admiral's tulip garden. Someone may have forgotten to dot a few "i"'s.

*(JO exits.)*

**KAFFEE.** Hey, Sam, I think she was talkin' about you.

**SAM.** You think?

**WHITAKER.** The two of you, don't get cute down there. The Marines in Guantanamo are fanatical.

**KAFFEE.** About what?

**SANTIAGO.** *Dear Sir,*

**WHITAKER.** About being Marines.

*(Lights up on SANTIAGO.)*

**SANTIAGO.** My name is PFC William T. Santiago. I am a Marine stationed at Marine Barracks, Windward, Guantanamo Bay, Cuba. I am writing to inform you of my problems and to ask for your help. I have been mistreated since the very first day I arrived. I've been punished for passing out on runs when the doctor says I just have heat exhaustion. This is just one incident of mistreatment and I could say many more but I do not want to take more of your time than I am allowed to. I've written many letters and gotten no response back so I must try something else. I know of an illegal fenceline shooting that took place four nights ago. A member of my unit illegally discharged his weapon into Cuban territory. I will give his name in exchange for a transfer. I ask you to help me. Please, sir, I just need to be transferred out of RSC.

*(Lights up on* **JESSEP**'s *office.)*

**TOM.** Excuse me, sir, Captain Markinson and Lt. Kendrick to see you.

**JESSEP.** Thank you, Tom.

**MARKINSON.** Good morning, Colonel.

**JESSEP.** Matthew, Jon, have a seat.

**MARKINSON.** Thank you.

**JESSEP.** Ten-hundred hours, already hot enough to melt the brass off your collar. I just had a Navy guy in here telling me we're lucky. After all, it's "dry heat." Dry heat. It's a hundred and seven degrees outside, how am I supposed to feel about that. Matthew, you've been here the longest, is this about as hot as it gets or am I actually trapped in hell.

**MARKINSON.** This is as hot as it's been since maybe '84, Colonel.

**JESSEP.** '84 was pretty bad?

**MARKINSON.** Got up to 119 degrees.

**JESSEP.** "Capering half in smoke, and half in fire." *(pause)* Moby Dick. *(pause)* Jon, when I quote Melville, you don't have to nod your head up and down like you know what I'm talking about.

**KENDRICK.** Yes sir.

**JESSEP.** I'm not gonna regard you as less of a man because you're not well read.

**KENDRICK.** Thank you, sir.

**JESSEP.** I mean that Jon.

**KENDRICK.** I appreciate that, sir.

**JESSEP.** 119 degrees Fahrenheit.

**MARKINSON.** Yes sir.

**JESSEP.** You must've had Marines passing out right and left.

**MARKINSON.** No, the men were alright.

**JESSEP.** Nobody passed out?

**MARKINSON.** Not that I recall.

**JESSEP.** Nobody got dizzy or hyperventilated? No heat exhaustion?

**MARKINSON.** No sir.

**JESSEP.** Impressive.

**MARKINSON.** Yes sir.

**JESSEP.** You know why those Marines didn't pass out back in '84, Jonathan? Even though it was 119 degrees Fahrenheit by Captain Markinson's reckoning? You know why they stayed on the job?

**KENDRICK.** Why, sir?

**JESSEP.** 'Cause that's what they're fuckin' trained to do.

**KENDRICK.** Yes sir.

(**JESSEP** *tosses a stack of letters to* **MARKINSON.**)

**JESSEP.** Who the fuck is PFC William T. Santiago?

(*Lights up on brig.*)

**M.P.** Officer on deck, ten-hut.

(**DAWSON** *and* **DOWNEY** *come to attention as* **JO** *enters.*)

**JO.** Good morning, I'm Lt. Commander Galloway.

**DAWSON.** Ma'am, Lance Corporal Harold W. Dawson, ma'am. Marine Barracks, Rifle Security Company Windward.

**DOWNEY.** Ma'am, Private First Class Louden Downey, ma'am.

**JO.** Stand easy. I work for the Navy JAG Corps, I'm the one who had you guys brought up here. I wanted to stop in and see if there was anything you needed. (*pause*) Or any questions you wanted to ask. (*pause*) It's natural for you to be a little confused or frightened...and so anything I can help you with...any questions you might have...

**DOWNEY.** Ma'am, permission to speak?

**JO.** Go ahead.

**DOWNEY.** I got some Spidermans and some Batmans sittin' in my footlocker. Somebody'll dog 'em for sure if they're not secured, ma'am.

**JO.** You think this is a joke?

**DOWNEY.** Ma'am, no ma'am!!

**JO.** *(to* **DAWSON***)* What about you, is this a joke?

**DAWSON.** No ma'am, it's not a joke, ma'am.

**DOWNEY.** I apologize to the Commander, ma'am. I didn't mean nothin'. About the books, ma'am, I didn't mean nothin'.

**JO.** You were read your Article 31 rights, did you understand them?

**DAWSON.** Yes ma'am.

**JO.** *(to* **DOWNEY***)* Did you understand them?

**DOWNEY.** Yes ma'am.

**JO.** Say you understand them.

**DOWNEY.** Ma'am, I understand them, ma'am.

**JO.** *(calling out)* Can I get an M.P. *(to* **DAWSON***)* I'm gonna talk to Private Downey alone for a moment.

*(An* **M.P.** *appears.)*

Would you take Corporal Dawson into a holding room?
**M.P.** Aye, aye Commander.

*(But* **DAWSON** *doesn't move.)*

Alright, let's move.

*(***DAWSON** *still doesn't budge.)*

Hey, asshole! I said move it!

**DAWSON.** *(quietly)* Ma'am, permission to be dismissed.

**JO.** You're dismissed.

*(***DAWSON** *turns and exits, followed by the* **M.P.** *)*

*(***JO** *turns to* **DOWNEY.** **DOWNEY***'s scared as hell to be without* **DAWSON**.*)*

Hi.

*(beat)*

Your only living relative is Ginny Miller, your aunt on your mother's side, is that right?

*(beat)* Ginny Miller?

**DOWNEY.** Yes ma'am.

**JO.** She hasn't been contacted yet, would you like me to take care of that for you?

*(beat)*

I'll take care of that for you. *(pause)* Private, do you know why you're here?

**DOWNEY.** *(pause)* Ma'am, this is where the guard told me to stand.

**JO.** *(pause)* Louden? May I call you Louden?

**DOWNEY.** Yes ma'am.

**JO.** Do you know where you are? *(pause)* Do you know why you've been arrested?

**DOWNEY.** Willy died, ma'am.

**JO.** Why? *(pause)* Was it an accident or did you mean to do it? *(pause)* Louden, I know about code reds.

**DOWNEY.** *(very nervous now)* Ma'am?

**JO.** I can help you. Was it a code red?

**DOWNEY.** I don't need those comic books, ma'am. You can have 'em if you like.

**JO.** You've gotta talk to somebody, Louden. They're gonna try and pin you with intent, they're gonna try to say this was a retaliation for Santiago snitching on Dawson with regard to the fenceline shooting.

*(beat)*

Which it wasn't, was it?

**DOWNEY.** Ma'am, permission to speak?

**JO.** Sure.

**DOWNEY.** Are you our lawyer, ma'am?

**JO.** I'm – no. *(pause)* I'm a lawyer, but I'm not the one representing you.

**DOWNEY.** Captain Markinson told us to talk to our lawyer ma'am. That's what he told us to do.

*(Lights up on softball field.)*

*(**KAFFEE** is calling out to unseen players.)*

**KAFFEE.** Alright, man on first, one down, let's go for two. *(to someone a little closer)* Hit a few out to Sherby.

*(calling out)* Get your glove down, Sherby, you gotta get your glove down. Pick up some dirt with that ball. Let's do it again. Man on first, one down.

*(**JO** enters.)*

**JO.** Excuse me.

**KAFFEE.** One second. *(calling out)* You gotta trust me, Sherby. If you keep your eyes *open* while the ball is coming toward you, your chances of catching the ball increase by a factor of ten. *(to **JO**)* You wanna suit up? We need all the help we can get.

**JO.** No thanks. I can't throw and catch things.

**KAFFEE.** That's too bad, 'cause neither can any of –

**JO.** I wanted to talk to you about Dawson and Downey.

**KAFFEE.** *(pause)* I've done something wrong, haven't I?

**JO.** I'm wondering why two guys have been in a cell since this morning while their lawyer is outside hitting a ball.

**KAFFEE.** We need the practice.

**JO.** That wasn't funny.

**KAFFEE.** It was a little funny.

**JO.** Lieutenant, would you feel very insulted if I asked your supervisor to recommend that different counsel be assigned?

**KAFFEE.** Why?

**JO.** I'm not sure how to say this without possibly hurting your feelings, but I don't think you're fit to handle this defense.

**KAFFEE.** You don't even know me. Ordinarily it takes some-one hours to discover I'm not fit to handle a defense.

*(beat)*

I think there are people who would've thought that was funny.

**JO.** I do know you. And I know who your father was. And I know you went to Harvard Law on a Navy scholarship and that you're probably just treading water for the three years you've gotta serve, just kinda laying low till you can get out and get a real job. And if that's the case, that's fine, I won't tell anyone. But my feeling is that if this case is handled in the fast-food, slick-ass, Persian Bazaar manner with which you seem to handle everything else, something's gonna get missed. And I wouldn't be doing my job if I allowed Dawson and Downey to spend anymore time in jail than absolutely necessary because their attorney had pre-determined the path of least resistance.

**KAFFEE.** *(pause)* I may be picking the wrong time to ask you this but are you seeing anyone right now? – 'cause I think you and I would be perfect together. It's clear that you respect me and that's the foundation for any solid–

**JO.** Shut up.

**KAFFEE.** Yes ma'am.

**JO.** I don't think your clients murdered anybody.

**KAFFEE.** Well, we're gonna have to take their word for it, don't you think?

**JO.** I mean I don't think there was any intent.

**KAFFEE.** The doctor's report says Santiago died of asphyxiation brought on by acute lactic acidosis, and that the nature of the acidosis strongly suggests poisoning. I don't know what most of that means, but it sounds pretty bad.

**JO.** The doctor's wrong.

**KAFFEE.** That's a relief. I was afraid I wouldn't be able to use the Liar, Liar, Pants on Fire defense.

**JO.** Kaffee –

**KAFFEE.** Look, rest assured, I'm completely on top of the situation with Dawson and Donnelly.

**JO.** Downey.

**KAFFEE.** –Downey.

**JO.** I'll speak to your supervisor.

**KAFFEE.** I understand. You go straight up Pennsylvania Avenue, it's the big white house with the pillars in front.

**JO.** Thank you.

**KAFFEE.** I don't think you'll have much luck, though. I was detailed by Division, remember? Somebody over there is under the impression I'm a good lawyer. So while I appreciate your interest and admire your enthusiasm, I think I can handle things myself at this point.

**JO.** Do you know what a code red is?

*(In* **JESSEP***'s office,* **MARKINSON** *puts down* **SANTIAGO***'s letter.)*

**MARKINSON.** I'm appalled, sir.

**KAFFEE.** No, I don't.

**JO.** Find out.

*(Lights up on* **JESSEP***'s office.)*

**JESSEP.** You're appalled?

**MARKINSON.** Yes sir.

**JESSEP.** That's pretty strong language, Matthew, I mean maybe you better cool off before you work yourself into a lather. You're appalled? Santiago's written letters to everyone but Santa Clause complaining about his treatment, he's broken the chain of command, he's threatened to rat out a member of his unit, a member of his squad for Christ's sake, to say nothing of the fact that he's a U.S. Marine and it would appear that he can't run from here to there without collapsing from heat exhaustion. What the hell's going on over at Windward, Matthew?

**MARKINSON.** Colonel, I think it might be more appropriate if this discussion were held in private.

**KENDRICK.** That won't be necessary, Colonel. I can handle the problem.

**MARKINSON.** The way you handled Curtis Barnes? You're doing something wrong, and–

**KENDRICK.** My methods of leadership are what brought me to this base.

**MARKINSON.** Don't interrupt me, I'm still your superior officer.

**JESSEP.** And I'm yours, Matthew. Now what are we gonna do about this?

**MARKINSON.** I think we've gotta transfer Santiago, sir. Right away. Now.

**JESSEP.** Transfer Santiago.

**MARKINSON.** Yes sir.

**JESSEP.** I suppose you're right. I suppose that's the thing to do. Wait. Wait. I've got a better idea. Let's transfer the whole squad off the base. We better do that. Let's – on second thought – Windward. The whole Windward division, let's transfer 'em off the base. Jon, go on out there and get those boys down off the fence, they're packin' their bags.
*(calling out)* Tom!

**TOM.** *(entering)* Sir!

**JESSEP.** Get me the President, we're surrendering our position in Cuba.

**TOM.** Yes sir.

**JESSEP.** Wait a minute, Tom. Don't call the President. Maybe that's the wrong thing to do. Maybe you should let us consider this for a moment. You're dismissed.

*(**TOM** exits.)*

Maybe, instead of giving up because a Marine made a mistake, maybe we should train Santiago. What do you think, I'm just spitballing, but maybe, we as officers, have a responsibility to this country to see that the men and women charged with its security are properly trained professionals. And maybe we have that responsibility to the other members of the Corps. Yes. Yes. I'm certain I once read something like that. See? And now

I'm trying to think of how I might feel if a Marine got hurt or killed because a PFC in my command didn't know what the fuck he was doing. And this brief meditation has brought me around to the thinking that your suggestion of transferring Private Santiago, while expeditious, and certainly painless, might not be, in a manner of speaking, the American way.

*(beat)*

Santiago stays where he is, we're gonna train the lad. Jon, you're in charge. Santiago doesn't make 4.6-4.6 on his next procon report, I'm gonna blame you. Then I'm gonna kill you.

**MARKINSON.** You're making a mistake, Colonel.

**JESSEP.** Matthew, I believe I will have that word in private with you now. Jon, that's all. Why don't you and I have lunch at the OClub, we can talk about how to train the Private.

**KENDRICK.** I'd be delighted sir.

**JESSEP.** Dismissed.

*(**KENDRICK** exits.)*

Matthew, sit, please.

*(**MARKINSON** sits.)*

What do you think of Kendrick?

**MARKINSON.** Nathan, this isn't personal. My opinion of Jon Kendrick isn't –

**JESSEP.** I think he's kind of a weasel myself.

**MARKINSON.** Yes sir.

**JESSEP.** But he's an awfully good officer, and in the end we see eye to eye on the best way to run a Marine Corps unit. We're in the business of saving lives, Matthew. With every degree that we allow ourselves to fall off the mark of perfection, more people die. And I believe that taking a Marine who's a weak link and packing him off to another assignment without giving him the proper training is the same as sending a kid into the jungle with a weapon that backfires.

(**MARKINSON** *starts to stand.*)

**JESSEP.** *(cont.)* Matthew. Siddown.

(*beat*)

I'm younger than you are, Matthew, and if that's a source of tension or embarrassment for you, well, I don't give a shit. We're in the business of saving lives. Don't ever question my orders in front of another officer.

(*Lights up on brig.*)

**DAWSON.** Officer on deck, ten-hut.

(**DAWSON** *and* **DOWNEY** *come to attention as* **KAFFEE** *and* **SAM** *enter.*)

**KAFFEE.** Hi.

**DAWSON.** Sir, Lance Corporal Harold W. Dawson, sir.

**KAFFEE.** Someone hasn't been working and playing well with others, Harold.

**DOWNEY.** Sir, Private First Class Louden Downey, sir.

**KAFFEE.** I'm Daniel Kaffee, I'm your attorney. This is Sam Weinberg, he's from the A.C. Nielson media research, he's gonna talk to you about viewer preferences in the Caribbean Command. You can sit down.

(**KAFFEE** *takes their confessions out of his briefcase and shows them to* **DAWSON** *and* **DOWNEY**.)

Is this your signature?

**DAWSON.** Yes sir.

**KAFFEE.** You don't have to call me sir. *(to* **DOWNEY***)* Is this your signature?

**DOWNEY.** Sir, yes sir.

**KAFFEE.** And you certainly don't have to do it twice in one sentence. What's a code red?

**DAWSON.** Sir?

**KAFFEE.** Really, you don't have to call me sir. What's a code red?

**DAWSON.** Sir, a code red is a disciplinary engagement.

**KAFFEE.** What's that?

**DAWSON.** Sir, a Marine falls out of line, it's the responsibility of the men in his unit to get him back on track.

**KAFFEE.** *(to SAM)* Did you know this?

**SAM.** It's like a hazing.

**KAFFEE.** *(to DAWSON)* What's a garden variety code red?

**DAWSON.** Sir?

**KAFFEE.** Harold, you say sir, I turn around and look for my father. Garden variety, typical, what's a basic code red?

**DAWSON.** Sir, a Marine has refused to bathe on a regular basis. The men in his squad would give him a G.I. shower.

**KAFFEE.** What's that?

**DAWSON.** Scrub brushes, brillo pads, steel wool...

**SAM.** Beautiful.

**KAFFEE.** Was the attack on Santiago a code red?

**DAWSON.** Yes sir.

**KAFFEE.** Does he ever talk?

**DAWSON.** Sir, Private Downey will answer any direct questions you ask him, sir.

**KAFFEE.** Swell. It says in the report you guys deny putting poison on the rag. What was it you were gonna do?

**DOWNEY.** Sir?

**KAFFEE.** What was the code red supposed to be?

**DOWNEY.** We were gonna shave his head, sir. We were just gonna shave his head.

**KAFFEE.** When all of a sudden?

**DOWNEY.** We saw blood dripping out of his mouth. We pulled the tape off his mouth and pulled the gag out, sir.

**KAFFEE.** Was there more blood?

**DOWNEY.** All down his face, sir. And then Corporal Dawson called the ambulance.

**KAFFEE.** *(to DAWSON)* You called the ambulance?

**DAWSON.** Yes sir.

**KAFFEE.** That wasn't in the report.

**DAWSON.** We were never asked about it, sir.

**KAFFEE.** Did anyone see you call the ambulance?

**DAWSON.** No sir.

**KAFFEE.** Were you there when the ambulance got there?

**DAWSON.** Yes sir. That's when we were taken under arrest.

**KAFFEE.** I want to tell you about something called attorney/
client privilege. It means you can say anything you
want to us in here and we're not allowed to repeat it
without your permission. It's against the law. We took
an oath. You took the oath, didn't you, Sam?

**SAM.** Yeah.

**KAFFEE.** Sam took the oath. Harold, did you assault
Santiago with the intent of killing him?

**DAWSON.** No sir.

**KAFFEE.** What was your intent?

**DAWSON.** To train him, sir.

**KAFFEE.** Train him to do what?

**DAWSON.** Train him to think of his unit before himself.
Train him to respect the code, sir.

**SAM.** What's the code?

**KAFFEE.** Who cares?

**SAM.** No, what's the code?

**DAWSON.** Unit, Corps, God, Country.

**SAM.** I beg your pardon?

**DAWSON.** Our code is Unit, Corps, God, Country, sir. That's
our code, sir.

**SAM.** It seems to be working out well for you.

**KAFFEE.** We'll be back. Is there anything you guys need?
Books, paper, cigarettes, a ham sandwich?

**DAWSON.** Sir. No, thank you, sir.

**KAFFEE.** Harold, there's a concept I think you better start
warming up to.

**DAWSON.** Sir?

KAFFEE. I'm the only friend you've got.

*(Lights up on* ROSS.*)*

ROSS. Dan Kaffee.

KAFFEE. Smilin' Jack Ross.

ROSS. I hope for Dawson and Downey's sake you practice law better than you play softball.

KAFFEE. Unfortunately for Dawson and Downey, I don't do anything better than I play softball. What are we lookin' at?

ROSS. They plead to Manslaughter, I'll drop the conspiracy and the bad conduct. Twenty years, they'll be home in half that time.

KAFFEE. I want twelve.

ROSS. Can't do it.

KAFFEE. They called the ambulance, Jack.

ROSS. I don't care if they called the Avon Lady, they killed a Marine.

KAFFEE. The rag was tested for poison. The autopsy, lab report, even the initial E.R. and C.O.D. reports all say the same thing: Maybe, maybe not.

ROSS. The Chief of Internal Medicine at the Guantanamo Bay Naval Hospital says he's sure.

KAFFEE. What do you know about code reds?

**(ROSS** *smiles and shakes his head.)*

ROSS. Oh shit.

*(beat)*

Are we off the record?

**(KAFFEE** *smiles and shakes his head.)*

KAFFEE. No. We're not.

ROSS. *(pause)* I'll give you the twelve years, but before you go getting yourself into trouble down there, you should know this: The platoon Commander, Lt. Jonathan Kendrick, had a meeting with the men and specifically told them not to touch Santiago.

(**KAFFEE** *holds for a moment.* **DAWSON** *and* **DOWNEY** *neglected to mention this. He picks up his briefcase.*)

**KAFFEE.** I'll see you when I get back.

**ROSS.** Do we have a deal?

**KAFFEE.** Talk to me when I get back.

(*Lights up on* **KAFFEE***'s office.*)

(**JO** *is sitting at the desk as* **KAFFEE** *enters.*)

Come on in.

**JO.** Thank you.

**KAFFEE.** Any luck getting me replaced?

**JO.** Is there anyone in this command that you don't either drink or play softball with?

**KAFFEE.** Say, Commander –

**JO.** You can call me Jo.

**KAFFEE.** Jo, I have no inbred hostility toward you, I really don't, but if you ever speak to a client of mine again without my permission, I'll have you disbarred.

**JO.** I had authorization.

**KAFFEE.** You had authorization from where?

**JO.** Downey's closest living relative, Ginny Miller, his aunt on his mother's side.

**KAFFEE.** You got authorization from Aunt Ginny?

**JO.** I gave her a call, I thought she might be concerned. Perfectly within my province.

**KAFFEE.** You got authorization from Aunt Ginny.

**JO.** Very nice woman, we talked for about an hour.

**KAFFEE.** Does Aunt Ginny have a barn? We can hold the trial there. I can sew the costumes and maybe his uncle Goober could be the judge.

**JO.** More good news. My office has been encouraging me to get out of the district more to observe how our lawyers are working in the field. Guess where I'm going?

**KAFFEE.** A target range?

**JO.** I'm going down to Cuba with you tomorrow.

**KAFFEE.** And the hits just keep on comin'.

*(Lights up on SAM's apt.)*

*(SAM comes out with two bottles of beer and hands one to KAFFEE.)*

**SAM.** She's asleep now. When Laura gets back, you're my witness. The baby spoke. My daughter said a word.

**KAFFEE.** She made a sound, I'm not sure it was a word.

**SAM.** Oh come on, it was a word.

**KAFFEE.** Okay.

**SAM.** You heard her. The girl sat here, pointed, and said "Pa." She did. She said "Pa."

**KAFFEE.** She was pointing at a doorknob.

**SAM.** That's right. Pointing, as if to say "Pa, look, a doorknob."

**KAFFEE.** Jack Ross came to see me today. He offered me twelve years.

**SAM.** That's what you wanted.

**KAFFEE.** I know, and I'll...I guess, I mean –

*(beat)*

I'll take it.

**SAM.** So?

**KAFFEE.** It took about 45 seconds. He barely put up a fight.

**SAM.** Danny, take the twelve years, it's a gift.

**KAFFEE.** You don't believe their story, do you? You think they should go to jail for the rest of their lives.

**SAM.** I believe every word they said. And I think they should go to jail for the rest of their lives.

*(KAFFEE gets up.)*

**KAFFEE.** I'll see you tomorrow.

**SAM.** Remember to wear your whites, it's hot down there.

**KAFFEE.** I don't look good in whites.

**SAM.** Nobody looks good in whites, but we're going to Cuba in July. You got Dramamine?

**KAFFEE.** Dramamine keeps you cool?

**SAM.** You get sick when you fly.

**KAFFEE.** I get sick when I fly 'cause I'm afraid of crashing into a large mountain, I don't think Dramamine'll help.

**SAM.** I got some oregano, I hear that works pretty good.

**KAFFEE.** Yeah.

*(He starts to leave, but turns back.)*

**KAFFEE.** You know, Ross said the strangest thing to me right before I left. He said, "The platoon Commander, Lt. Jonathan Kendrick, had a meeting with the men, and specifically told them not to touch Santiago."

**SAM.** So?

**KAFFEE.** I never mentioned Kendrick. I don't even know who he is.

*(beat)*

What the hell.

*(baby cry)*

I'll see you tomorrow.

*(Lights up on platoon meeting.)*

*(***KENDRICK*** enters.)*

**DUNN.** Ten-hut.

**KENDRICK.** Squad leaders, front and center. Report. Dunn Sir, Corporal Dunn, Alpha Squad present, sir.

**HAMMAKER.** Corporal Hammaker, Bravo's present.

**HOWARD.** Sir, Corporal Howard, Charlie's present.

**DAWSON.** Sir, Lance Corporal Dawson. Delta's present less two.

**KENDRICK.** Private Santiago's been excused from this meeting, where's Private Downey.

**DAWSON.** Downey radioed into the switch, sir, his jeep blew out. He and pick-up are making it back by foot.

**KENDRICK.** Pass on my words to Private Downey. Anything I say to the squad leaders at this meeting is to be considered a direct order to the members of your squads, is that clear.

**ALL.** Sir, yes sir!

**KENDRICK.** Revelations II: I know thy works and thy labour and how thou canst not bare them which are evil. And thou hast tried them which say they are apostles and has found them to be liars. If you have a problem and you're a PFC, who do you take that problem to?

**ALL.** Sir, your corporal, sir!

**KENDRICK.** If you are a corporal and you have a problem, who do you take that problem to?

**ALL.** Sir, your sergeant, sir!

**KENDRICK.** Private Santiago of Delta squad has laid waste our priorities and made wretched our code, Priorities:

**ALL.** Unit, Corps, God, Country!

**KENDRICK.** Code:

**ALL.** Unit, Corps, God, Country!

**KENDRICK.** What are we here to fight for?!

**ALL.** Unit, Corps, God, Country!

**KENDRICK.** What are we here to fight for!?

**ALL.** Unit, Corps, God, Country!!!

**KENDRICK.** Do you need someone from outside this unit to show you how to be good?

**ALL.** Sir, no sir!

**KENDRICK.** Do you need someone from outside this unit to show you how to be right?!

**ALL.** Sir, no sir!

**KENDRICK.** Corporal Dunn!

**DUNN.** Sir!

**KENDRICK.** You think you and the boys of Alpha Squad could show Santiago how to be right?

**DUNN.** Sir, yes sir.

**KENDRICK.** Anybody in Alpha goes near him, you'll answer to me, is that clear?

**DUNN.** Sir?

**KENDRICK.** Is it clear?

**DUNN.** Sir yes sir.

**KENDRICK.** Alpha's dismissed.

(**DUNN** *exits.*)

Corporal Hammaker.

**HAMMAKER.** Sir!

**KENDRICK.** How 'bout my brave men of Bravo. I bet I turn this over to your boys and Santiago's a Marine by sunrise, am I right?

**HAMMAKER.** Sir yes sir!

**KENDRICK.** Bravo touches him and you'll all be fillin' sandbags till you beg for mercy. Dismissed.

(**HAMMAKER** *exits.*)

Corporal Howard.

**HOWARD.** Sir!

**KENDRICK.** I have two things to say to you. The first is that I believe in my heart that you and the men of Charlie Squad are outstanding Marines, and that your influence over the Private would be invaluable. The second is that the government of the United States maintains a military installation in the Arctic Circle, and you and the men of Charlie will find yourselves scraping icicles off of igloos in a heartbeat if you so much as look funny at the Private, is that clear?

**HOWARD.** Yes sir!

**KENDRICK.** No code reds, is that clear?

**HOWARD.** Sir, yes sir!

**KENDRICK.** No code reds, is that clear??!!

**HOWARD.** Sir, yes sir!!

**KENDRICK.** No code reds, is that clear??!!!

**HOWARD.** Sir, yes sir!!!

**KENDRICK.** Dismissed.

(**HOWARD** *exits.* **KENDRICK** *turns to* **DAWSON**.)

**KENDRICK.** Lance Corporal Dawson.

**DAWSON.** Sir.

(*blackout*)

*(A platoon of* **MARINES** *is heard chanting.)*

**MARINES.** Lift your head and lift it high

LIFT YOUR HEAD AND LIFT IT HIGH

Delta Company's passin' by

DELTA COMPANY'S PASSIN' BY

I don't know but I been told

I DON'T KNOW BUT I BEEN TOLD

All Marines are mighty bold

ALL MARINES ARE MIGHTY BOLD

*(The chanting continues over the sounds of jets taking off and landing.)*

Sound off!

ONE TWO!

Sound off!

THREE FOUR!

Sound off!

ONE TWO THREE FOUR

ONE TWO –

THREE FOUR!

*(Lights up on the airstrip.)*

**(HOWARD** *meets* **KAFFEE, JO,** *and* **SAM**. **KAFFEE** *and* **SAM** *are wearing whites,* **JO** *is in khakis. They shout over the noise of the jets.)*

**HOWARD.** Lieutenants Kaffee and Weinberg?

**KAFFEE.** *(shouting)* Yeah!

**JO.** I'm Commander Galloway.

**HOWARD.** Corporal Howard, ma'am, I'm to escort you to the Windward side of the base.

**JO.** Thank you.

**HOWARD.** I've got some camouflage jackets, sirs, I'll have to ask you both to put them on.

**KAFFEE.** Camouflage jackets?

**HOWARD.** Yes sir. Regulations. We'll be riding pretty close to the fence. Cubans see an officer wearin' white, they think it's someone they might want to take a shot at.

**KAFFEE.** Good call, Sam.

**HOWARD.** The jeep's right over there, ma'am. We'll just hop on the ferry and be there in no time.

**KAFFEE.** Whoa, whoa, we have to take a boat?

**HOWARD.** Yes sir, to get to the other side of the bay.

**KAFFEE.** Whitaker didn't say anything about a boat?

**HOWARD.** Is there a problem, sir?

**KAFFEE.** No. No problem. I'm just not crazy about boats, that's all.

**JO.** Jesus Christ Kaffee, you're in the Navy for cryin' out loud, you wanna get a hold of yourself?

**KAFFEE.** (*to* **HOWARD**) Nobody likes her very much.

**HOWARD.** Yes sir.

(*Lights up on* **JESSEP**'s *office.*)

(*The* **LAWYERS** *are being ushered in.*)

**JESSEP.** Nathan Jessep, come on in and siddown.

**KAFFEE.** Thank you. This is Commander Joanne Galloway, she's observing and evaluating.

**JO.** How do you do?

**JESSEP.** Pleased to meet you, Commander.

**KAFFEE.** Sam Weinberg, he has no responsibilities here whatsoever.

**JESSEP.** I've asked Captain Markinson and Lt. Kendrick to join us. Matthew's my second in command and Jonathan's X.O. for the Windward side.

**MARKINSON.** Lt. Kaffee, I had the pleasure of meeting your father once. I was a teenager and he spoke at my high school.

(**KAFFEE** *smiles and nods.*)

**JESSEP.** Lionel Kaffee?

**KAFFEE.** Yes sir.

**JESSEP.** Well, Jimminy Goddamn Cricket. Jon, you're too young to know, but this man's dad once made a lot of enemies down in your neck of the woods. Jefferson v. Madison County School District. Folks down there said it was all right for kids to say the Lord's prayer in the classroom and Lionel Kaffee said no, no it wasn't. Tell you something else: if Adlai Stevenson'd ever been elected, you'd be sittin' with the son of the Attorney General. How the hell is your dad?

**KAFFEE.** I beg your pardon?

**JESSEP.** Still tryin' to overthrow the government?

**KAFFEE.** Not any longer, sir.

**JESSEP.** Oh no. Don't tell me he passed away.

**KAFFEE.** Yes sir.

**JESSEP.** I'm sorry, son.

**KAFFEE.** Thank you, sir. It was seven years ago.

**JESSEP.** *(pause)* Well…don't I feel like the fuckin' asshole.

**KAFFEE.** Not at all, sir.

**JESSEP.** What can we do for you, Danny?

**KAFFEE.** Not much at all, sir, I'm afraid. This is really a formality more than anything else. The JAG Corps insists that I interview all the relevant witnesses.

**JO.** The JAG Corps can be demanding that way.

**KAFFEE.** It shouldn't take more than an hour.

**JESSEP.** Jon, check your watch. *(to **KAFFEE**)* Go.

   *(Lights up on **SANTIAGO**'s room.)*

   *(**SANTIAGO**, his hands and feet tied with rope, is dragged on by **DOWNEY**. **DAWSON** comes into the scene.)*

**SANTIAGO.** HEEELLLP MEEEEE!!!

   *(**DAWSON** holds **SANTIAGO**'s head as **DOWNEY** stuffs a piece of white cloth into his mouth.)*

**DOWNEY.** You're lucky it's us, Willy. Could be worse. Could be somebody else.

   *(Lights up on **JESSEP**'s office.)*

**KAFFEE.** Now on the morning of the sixth, you were contacted by an NIS agent who said that Santiago had
tipped him off to an illegal fenceline shooting.

**JESSEP.** Yes.

**KAFFEE.** Santiago was gonna reveal the person's name in
exchange for a transfer. Am I getting this right?

**JESSEP.** Yes.

**KAFFEE.** If there are any details that I'm leaving out, you
should feel free to speak up.

**JESSEP.** *(pause)* Thank you.

**KAFFEE.** Now it was at this point that you called Captain
Markinson and Lt. Kendrick into your office?

**JESSEP.** Yes.

**KAFFEE.** And what happened then?

**JESSEP.** We agreed that for his own safety, Santiago should
be transferred off the base.

**KAFFEE.** *(pause)* Santiago was gonna be transferred?

**JESSEP.** On the first available flight to the states. Six o'clock
the next morning. Six hours too late as it turned out.

(**KAFFEE** *nods.*)

**KAFFEE.** Yeah.

*(There's silence for a moment.)*

Alright, that's all I have. Thanks very much for your time.

**JO.** Wait a minute, I've got some questions.

**KAFFEE.** No you don't.

**JO.** Yes I do.

**KAFFEE.** No you don't.

**JO.** Colonel at three a.m., the attending physician,
Commander Stone, was unable to determine the cause
of death. At five a.m. he said it was poison. Do you
have any idea what might have persuaded him?

**JESSEP.** You'd have to ask Stone.

**JO.** Did you meet with the doctor between three and five.

**KAFFEE.** Jo –

**JESSEP.** Of course I met with the doctor. One of my men was dead.

**KAFFEE.** See? His man was dead. Let's go.

**JO.** Lt. Kendrick, do you think Santiago was murdered?

**KENDRICK.** I beg your pardon?

**JO.** I'm just curious. You knew all these men. Was Santiago murdered?

**KENDRICK.** Commander, I believe in God and in his son, Jesus Christ, and because I do, I can say this: Santiago is dead, and that's a tragedy. But he's dead because he had no code. He's dead because he had no honor. And God was watching.

**SAM.** *(to KAFFEE)* How do you feel about that theory?

**KAFFEE.** Sounds good. Let's go.

**KENDRICK.** I don't like you people.

**SAM.** Look at this, another Christmas card I'm not gonna get.

**JO.** Colonel Jessep, have you ever heard the term "Code Red"?

**KAFFEE.** Commander –

**JESSEP.** I was under the impression Lt. Kaffee was leading this investigation.

**JO.** It's an easy mistake to make.

**KAFFEE.** Colonel, I apologize, she wasn't –

**JO.** Have you ever heard the term code red, sir?

**JESSEP.** I've heard the term, yes.

**JO.** Colonel, this past February you received a cautionary memo from the Commander in Chief of the Atlantic Fleet warning that the practice of code reds was not to be condoned by officers.

**JESSEP.** I submit to you that whoever wrote that memo has never served on the working end of a Soviet-made Cuban AK-47 Assault Rifle. However, the directive having come from the Commander, I gave it its due attention. What's your point, Joanne?

**KAFFEE.** She has no point. She often has no point. It's part of her charm. We're outa here. Thank you.

**JO.** My point is that what looks like pre-meditated murder may have just been a botched up code red. Do code reds still happen on this base, Colonel?

**KAFFEE.** Jo, the Colonel doesn't need to answer that.

**JO.** Yes, he does.

**KAFFEE.** No, he really doesn't.

**JO.** Yeah, he really does. Colonel?

**JESSEP.** You know, it just hit me. She outranks you, Danny.

**KAFFEE.** Yes sir.

**JESSEP.** I want to tell you something, and listen up, 'cause I mean this: There is nothing sexier on heaven and earth than a woman you have to salute in the morning. Promote 'em all I say, 'cause this is true: If you've never gotten a blow job from a superior officer, than you are letting the best of life just pass you by.

**JO.** Colonel, the practice of code reds is still going on on this base, isn't it?

**KAFFEE.** Jo, goddamit –

**JESSEP.** You see, my problem is, of course, that I'm a Colonel. I'll just have to keep takin' cold showers till they elect some gal President.

**JO.** I need an answer to my question, sir.

**JESSEP.** You'll get an answer.

**JO.** I need it now, sir.

**JESSEP.** Take caution in your tone Commander, I'm a fair guy, but this fucking heat is making me absolutely crazy. You want to know about code reds? On the record I tell you I discourage the practice in accordance with the Commander's directive. Off the record I tell you that they're an invaluable part of close infantry training, and if they happen to go on without my knowledge, so be it. I run my unit how I run my unit. You want to investigate me, roll the dice and take your chances. It's not like you're gonna come down here, flash a badge, and make me nervous. I eat my breakfast 80 yards away from 4000 Cubans who are trained to kill me.

*(A moment of silence before − )*

**KAFFEE.** Let's go.

**MARKINSON.** The corporal's got the jeep outside. He'll take you back to the flightline.

**KAFFEE.** Thank you. Colonel, I'll just need a copy of that transfer order.

**JESSEP.** What's that?

**KAFFEE.** Santiago's transfer order. You guys have paperwork on that kind of thing. I just need it for the file.

**JESSEP.** For the file.

**KAFFEE.** Yeah.

**JESSEP.** *(pause)* Of course you can have a copy of the transfer order. For the file. I'm here to help anyway I can.

**KAFFEE.** Thank you.

**JESSEP.** You believe that, don't you, Danny? That I'm here to help any way I can?

**KAFFEE.** Sure.

**JESSEP.** The corporal can run you by personnel on your way to the flightline. You can have all the transfer orders you want.

**KAFFEE.** *(to* JO *and* SAM*)* Let's go.

**JESSEP.** But you have to ask me nicely.

**KAFFEE.** *(pause)* I beg your pardon?

**JESSEP.** You have to ask me nicely. I don't mind the bullets and the bombs and the blood, Danny. I don't mind the heat and the stress and the fear. I don't want money and I don't want medals. What I do want is for you to stand there and in that faggoty white uniform and with your Harvard mouth extend me some fuckin' courtesy. You gotta ask me nicely.

**SAM.** *(pause)* Don't do it, Danny.

**KAFFEE.** Colonel, if it's not too much trouble, I'd like a copy of the transfer order. Sir.

(**JESSEP** *smiles.*)

**JESSEP.** No problem.

*(The* LAWYERS *exit.)*

JESSEP. *(after a moment)* "First thing we do, let's kill all the lawyers."

MARKINSON. *(beat)* It's Shakespeare. Colonel –

JESSEP. I hate casualties, Matthew. A Marine smothers a grenade and saves his platoon, that Marine's doing his job. There are casualties. Even in victory. The fabric of the base, the foundation of the unit, the spirit of the Corps, these are things worth fighting for. And there's no one who doesn't know that who's ever made the decision to put on the uniform. I hate casualties.

*(pause)*

Dawson and Downey, they're smothering a grenade.

MARKINSON. Just the same, sir, if I were you, I'd get myself a lawyer.

*(blackout)*

*(We hear a platoon of* MARINES *chanting.)*

MARINES. What are you gonna do when you get back?
WHAT ARE YOU GONNA DO WHEN YOU GET BACK?
Take a shower and hit the rack!
TAKE A SHOWER AND HIT THE RACK!
Oh no
NOT ME
Oh no
NOT US
WHAT ARE WE GONNA DO WHEN WE GET BACK?
POLISH UP FOR A SNEAK ATTACK!

*(Lights up on brig.)*

DAWSON. Officer on deck, ten-hut.

*(KAFFEE enters.)*

KAFFEE. Why did you care that Santiago was writing a letter?

DAWSON. Sir?

**KAFFEE.** I want to know why you cared.

**DAWSON.** It was a code red, sir.

**KAFFEE.** Colonel Jessep thinks you're fulla shit. He doesn't think you were trying to train Santiago, he thinks you were trying to kill him.

**DOWNEY.** That's not true, sir –

**KAFFEE.** What's true? Why did you care?

**DAWSON.** It was a code red, sir.

**KAFFEE.** 4000 men on that base, none of them went into Santiago's room that night.

**DAWSON.** I was his squad leader, sir. It was my job.

**KAFFEE.** He was screwin' up every day for eight months, you never gave him a code red before that night. Why did you care that night?

**DAWSON.** Santiago broke the chain of –

**KAFFEE.** Not you. Him. Why did you care?

**DOWNEY.** Sir, Private Santiago broke the –

**KAFFEE.** No, no, I don't want to hear about your chain of command, I don't want to hear about loyalty, I don't want to hear about your bozo code of honor. Why did you give him a code red?

**DOWNEY.** Private Santiago broke –

**KAFFEE.** *Did you hear what I just said??!!*

**DOWNEY.** Private Santiago needed to learn how to –

**KAFFEE.** Why did you give him a code red?!!

**DOWNEY.** We have a responsibility to –

**KAFFEE.** Bullshit!! Why did you do it??!!!

**DAWSON.** *Because God was watching!!*

(*silence*)

**KAFFEE.** (*quietly*) What did Kendrick say to you?

(*Lights up on* **KENDRICK**.)

**KENDRICK.** God is watching, Lance Corporal Dawson. And he helps those who help themselves. And so do I. Get your house in order, Lance Corporal. Unit, Corps, God, Country...and duty to self simply isn't part of the equation. Get your house in order, so that these men can believe in you again. Get your house in order...so that the Lord our God can look down and say "There is a United States Marine, and I will stand at his side." Get your house in order...and don't let anyone ever tell you we're not at war.

*(Lights up on brig.)*

**KAFFEE.** You were given an order.

**DAWSON.** Yes sir.

**KAFFEE.** Kendrick ordered the code red.

**DAWSON.** Yes sir.

**KAFFEE.** He told every other man at that meeting not to touch him, then he ordered you two to – I've gotta talk to the prosecutor. You mind telling me why the hell you never mentioned this before?

**DAWSON.** You didn't ask us, sir.

**KAFFEE.** Cutie-pie shit's not gonna win you a place in my heart corporal, I get paid no matter how much time you spend in jail.

**DAWSON.** Yes sir. I know you do, sir.

**KAFFEE.** Fuck you, Harold. *(pause)* I'll be back later.

*(Lights up outside brig.)*

**JO.** What'd they say?

**KAFFEE.** I want you to stop following me, I want you to get off my back, and I want you to get off this case.

**JO.** Markinson went U.A.

**KAFFEE.** *(beat)* What?

**JO.** Unauthorized Absence.

**KAFFEE.** I know what it means. When?

**JO.** Tonight after we left.

**KAFFEE.** I'll talk to him in the morning.

**JO.** I already tried. Nobody can find him. What'd they say?

**KAFFEE.** You already tried? Do you understand the meaning of interfering with a government investigation?!

**JO.** Yes I do, but I'm not, 'cause I'm now Louden Downey's attorney.

**KAFFEE.** What the hell are you talking about?

**JO.** Aunt Ginny. She feels like she's known me for years. She said she'd feel more comfortable if I were directly involved. Louden signed the papers a half hour ago. Don't worry, I'm not gonna make a motion for separation, you're lead counsel. I defer to your skills as a litigator. What'd they say?

**KAFFEE.** *(stunned)* You frighten me. I'm involved in a situation now in which the stakes couldn't be higher. I'm not gonna take time out to give tutorials in criminal procedure to an internal affairs *schoolgirl* who doesn't know what the fuck she's doing.

**JO.** I just melt when you sugar-talk me, Danny, what'd they say?

**KAFFEE.** Kendrick gave them an order.

**JO.** What do we do now?

**KAFFEE.** Find Jack Ross.

*(Lights up on conference room.)*

**ROSS.** You *talk* to the other guys in the platoon.

**KAFFEE.** I don't need to –

**ROSS.** Alpha, Bravo, Charlie, they all say the same thing!

**KAFFEE.** They weren't there. Kendrick dismissed the rest of the platoon. You talked to *Kendrick*.

**ROSS.** I already talked to Kendrick. I told you before you went *down* there. He denies *everything*.

**JO.** *(to KAFFEE)* He talked to Kendrick?

**KAFFEE.** Yeah, he –

**JO.** *(to ROSS)* You talked to Kendrick?

**KAFFEE.** I didn't think anything of it at the –

**JO.** *(to* **ROSS***)* Why did you think there was anything to deny?

**KAFFEE.** Jo –

**ROSS.** I had a suspicion.

**JO.** You had –

**KAFFEE.** It's not important now.

**JO.** You had a suspicion and you chose not to share it with anyone?

**ROSS.** It was just a – *(to* **KAFFEE***)* Who is this?

**KAFFEE.** Commander Galloway is Downey's attorney. She's very pleased to meet you.

**ROSS.** Ebeneezer Galloway?

**JO.** Look –

**ROSS.** You wanna charge me with something, ma'am?

**JO.** How are you getting information 12, 24, 48 hours before we –

**ROSS.** You wanna charge me with something?

**SAM.** Hey!! Everybody!! In the interest of justice. Take a deep knee bend.

*(Everyone calms down a moment.)*

**KAFFEE.** Jo, Lt. Ross didn't know about the order. 'Cause if he did and he hadn't told us, he knows he'd be violating about 14 articles of the code of ethics. As it is, he's got enough to worry about. God forbid our clients decide to plead not guilty and testify for the record that these things happen every day.

**ROSS.** Kendrick specifically told the men –

**KAFFEE.** And then he specifically told Dawson and Downey to shave his head.

**ROSS.** That's not what Kendrick said.

**KAFFEE.** Kendrick is crazy, and Kendrick is mean, and Kendrick is lying.

**ROSS.** You have proof?

**KAFFEE.** I have the defendants.

**ROSS.** And I have 23 men who aren't accused of murder and a Marine Lieutenant with four letters of commendation.

**KAFFEE.** Why did Markinson go U.A.?

**ROSS.** We'll never know.

**KAFFEE.** You don't think I can subpoena Markinson?

**ROSS.** You can try, but you won't find him.

**KAFFEE.** What are you talking about Jack?

**ROSS.** You know what Markinson did for the first 17 of his 21 years in the Corps? C.I.C., Danny, Counter-Intelligence. Markinson's gone. There is no Markinson.

*(The wind is taken out of KAFFEE's sails.)*

**ROSS.** Colonel Jessep's star is on the rise. They're giving me a lot of room to spare him embarrassment.

**KAFFEE.** *(pause)* How much room?

**ROSS.** I can knock it all down to assault and bad conduct. Two years. They're home in six months.

**JO.** Danny, he's got a P.R. problem and he can't afford to go to court.

*(KAFFEE says nothing.)*

**ROSS.** *(to KAFFEE)* Which is lucky for you 'cause you're turning green at the thought of it. Yes, taking this to court would be bad for me. It would be bad for the Corps and I'd be held responsible for how the officers were treated as witnesses. But *you* go to court, and the boys go away for 40 years.

**KAFFEE.** Jack, come on –

**ROSS.** Are we *clear* on that?! We *have* to be clear on that. Once we go outside this room, I have to put the hammer down. They'll be charged with the boatload: Murder, Conspiracy, Conduct Unbecoming. And in a courtroom, you lose this case. Please. I'm your friend, and I'm telling you, I think Kendrick's lying and I don't think your guys belong in jail. But I don't get to make that decision. I represent the People. Without passion. You see? And the people have a case.

*(pause)*

**ROSS.** *(cont.)* Tell 'em to plead to assault. All in all, it's not a bad week's work for the defense.

*(beat)*

That's the end of this negotiation. Nine o'clock tomorrow. I'll see you at the arraignment.

*(Lights up on brig.)*

**KAFFEE.** Okay. Here's the deal. I think you're gonna be happy. Plead guilty to assault, and the government prosecutor will recommend two years, with probation after six months.

**(DAWSON** *and* **DOWNEY** *say nothing.)*

"Wow, Kaffee, you're a good lawyer. How can we ever thank you?" Just doin' my job. Fellas, did you hear what I said? You're going home in six months.

*(beat)*

Fellas?

**DAWSON.** I'm afraid we can't do that, sir.

**KAFFEE.** Do what?

**DAWSON.** Make a deal, sir.

**KAFFEE.** What are you talking about?

**DAWSON.** We did nothing wrong, sir. We did our job. If that has consequences, then I accept them. But I won't say I'm guilty, sir.

**(KAFFEE** *looks at* **JO.)**

**KAFFEE.** Did you – *(to* **DAWSON** *and* **DOWNEY)** Did she put you up to this?

**JO.** No.

**DAWSON.** We have a code, sir.

**KAFFEE.** Well zippity-doo-dah! You plead not-guilty and you'll be in jail for the rest of your life. Do what I'm telling you and you're home in six months.

**DAWSON.** Permission to –

**KAFFEE.** Speak!

**DAWSON.** What do we do then, sir?

**KAFFEE.** When?

**DAWSON.** After six months. We'd get a dishonorable discharge, right?

**KAFFEE.** Probably.

**DAWSON.** What do we do then, sir? We didn't join the Corps 'cause we felt like it. We joined 'cause it was a life decision. We wanted to live by a code, sir. And we found it in the Corps. And now you're asking us to sign a piece of paper that says we have no honor. You're asking us to say we're not Marines. If the court decides what we did was wrong, I'll accept whatever punishment they give. But I believe I was right, sir. I believe I did my job. I won't dishonor myself, my unit, or the Corps, so that I can go home in six months.

*(beat)*

Sir.

**KAFFEE.** *(pause)* You guys are a freak show.

*(Lights up on* **KAFFEE**'s *office.)*

*(* **SAM, KAFFEE,** *and* **JO** *enter.)*

I'm not gonna talk to Dawson anymore. He doesn't like me, and he's gonna go to jail just to spite me. I want to get him a new lawyer.

**SAM.** Alright, you make a motion tomorrow at the arraignment. The judge'll ask for the plea, we'll move to an eight-oh-two conference and you can explain the situation.

**KAFFEE.** *(beat)* Then that's that.

**JO.** *(beat)* Yeah. One thing, though. When you ask the judge for new counsel, be sure and ask nicely.

**KAFFEE.** What do you want from me?

**JO.** I want you to let 'em be judged! I want you to stand up and make an argument!

**SAM.** An argument that didn't work for Calley at My Lai, and an argument that didn't work for the Nazis at Nuremberg.

**KAFFEE.** For Christsake, Sam, do you really think that's the same as two teenage Marines executing a routine order that they never believed would result in harm? These guys aren't the Nazis.

**JO.** Don't look now, Danny, but you're arguing a position.

**KAFFEE.** *(pause)* Yeah.

*(beat)*

Tomorrow morning I'll get them a new attorney.

**JO.** Why are you so afraid to be a lawyer?

**KAFFEE.** Look –

**JO.** Were Daddy's expectations really that high?

**SAM.** Hey!

*(**KAFFEE** stares at **JO** for a moment.)*

**KAFFEE.** Dawson and Downey'll have their day in court. But they'll have it with another lawyer.

**JO.** Another lawyer won't be good enough. They need you.

**KAFFEE.** Why?

**JO.** Because you know how to win. *(pause)* I know how to fight. But you know how to win.

**KAFFEE.** I know the law.

*(**JO** sees that it's over.)*

**JO.** *(pause)* You know nothing about the law. You're a used car salesman, Daniel. You're an ambulance chaser with a rank. Live with that.

*(**JO** exits.)*

*(**SAM** and **KAFFEE** are alone.)*

**KAFFEE.** Sam?

*(beat)*

Why does a junior grade with six months experience and a track record for plea bargaining get singled out to handle a murder case?

*(pause)*

Would it be to make sure it never sees the inside of a courtroom?

*(blackout)*

*(We hear the **MARINES** chanting.)*

**MARINES.** Up in the morning with the rising sun
UP IN THE MORNING WITH THE RISING SUN
Gonna run all day till the day is done
GONNA RUN ALL DAY TILL THE DAY IS DONE
Left right
ONE TWO
Go right
THREE FOUR
LEFT RIGHT
ONE TWO THREE FOUR
ONE TWO
THREE FOUR!

*(Lights up on **DAWSON**'s cell.)*

*(**DAWSON**'s asleep. **KAFFEE**'s been drinking a little. **DAWSON** wakes up.)*

**KAFFEE.** They've got you guys in separate cells now, huh?

**DAWSON.** Yes sir.

**KAFFEE.** *(pause)* You wanna hear a joke? *(pause)* You hear about the Japanese pilot who hated jazz? *(pause)* He bombed Pearl Bailey. *(pause)* I was ninety-nine percent sure you weren't gonna laugh at that.
*(He takes out a flask.)* You want some milk? Good for the teeth and bones.

**DAWSON.** No. Thank you, sir.

*(**KAFFEE** takes a drink and sits.)*

**KAFFEE.** Well...I don't know how else to say this...I think you gotta do it. Let me make a deal for you. It's nothing Harold, it's 6 months, it's a hockey season. *(pause)* I mean...in the end...what difference does it make?

**DAWSON.** Do you think we were right?

**KAFFEE.** It doesn't matter what I think.

**DAWSON.** Do you think we were right?

**KAFFEE.** It isn't a matter of right and wrong –

**DAWSON.** Yes it is. It always is. That's something people like you say, but it is. Do you think we're guilty?

**KAFFEE.** What do you mean people like me?

**DAWSON.** Do you think we're guilty?

**KAFFEE.** I think you'd lose.

**DAWSON.** You're such a coward, I can't believe they let you wear a uniform.

(**KAFFEE** *wheels around and punches* **DAWSON** *in the stomach.*)

**KAFFEE.** You're going to Levenworth and there's nothing I can do about it. I coulda gotten you six months. I'm not gonna feel responsible for you.
*(calling out)* M.P.!!

*(An* **M.P.** *appears.)*

*(to* **DAWSON***)* What happened to saluting an officer when he leaves the room?

(**DAWSON** *slowly puts his hands in his pockets.* **KAFFEE** *turns and leaves.)*

*(Lights up on courtroom.)*

*(The participants begin to file in:* **SERGEANT AT ARMS,** **M.P.***'s escorting* **DAWSON** *and* **DOWNEY, ROSS** *takes his place,* **SAM** *and* **JO** *enter and take their places at the defense table.* **KAFFEE** *takes his place just as* **RANDOLPH** *enters.)*

**SERGEANT AT ARMS.** Ten-hut.

*(All rise.)*

**RANDOLPH.** Alright, where are we?

**SERGEANT AT ARMS.** Docket number 411275, VR-5. United States versus Lance Corporal Harold W. Dawson and Private First Class Louden Downey. Defendants are charged with Murder in the Second Degree, Conspiracy to Commit Murder, and Conduct Unbecoming a United States Marine.

**RANDOLPH.** Does the defense wish to enter a plea?

KAFFEE. Yeah.

> *(stands)* They're not guilty.
>
> *(silence)*

RANDOLPH. Enter a plea of not-guilty for the defendants. We'll adjourn until ten-hundred, one week from today, at which time this court will re-convene as a general court-martial. I'll see counsel in my chambers. Now.

> (**RANDOLPH** *raps his gavel and stands.*)

SERGEANT AT ARMS. Ten-hut.

> *(The* **M.P.**'s *lead* **DAWSON** *and* **DOWNEY** *out.* **KAFFEE** *stops them.)*

KAFFEE. Say, boys?

DOWNEY. Yes sir.

KAFFEE. Don't look at me and say "Yes sir" like I just asked you if you cleaned the latrine. You're not in the Marines right now, you're in jail. Get some rest and don't speak to anyone but the three of us. They're dismissed.

> *(The* **M.P.**'s *take* **DAWSON** *and* **DOWNEY** *off. The room's empty except for the three lawyers.* **JO** *and* **SAM** *have been standing in a state of shock.)*

SAM. Danny –

KAFFEE. They were following an order.

SAM. An illegal order.

KAFFEE. You think these guys know what an illegal order is? *I* don't know what an illegal order is.

SAM. Any decent human being would've known you don't –

KAFFEE. They're not permitted to question orders. Period.

SAM. Then what's the secret? What are the magic words? I give orders every day and *nobody* follows them!

KAFFEE. We work where there are softball games and marching bands. They work where you gotta wear camouflage or you might get shot.

> *(And now* **KAFFEE** *can no longer stand the fact that* **JO**'s *been staring at him and smiling.)*

What are *you* lookin' at?

**JO.** What made you change your mind?

**KAFFEE.** Not you.

**SAM.** The law says you can't do what they did, it's as simple as that.

**KAFFEE.** It's not as simple as that. We're defense counsel, we position the truth, what'd they teach you.

**SAM.** To tell the truth, not position it.

**KAFFEE.** They taught you wrong.

**JO.** We're wasting time.

**KAFFEE.** Hey kitten? I'll decide how time is spent and how it's wasted. You got a problem with that, Downey can stand separate trial.

**JO.** You're still an asshole, you know.

**KAFFEE.** We'll work at my place every night, seven o'clock. Jo, before you come over tonight, pick up a carton of legal pads, a half dozen boxes of red pens, a half-dozen boxes of blue pens. Sam, get a couple of card tables and some desk lamps. I'm gonna start on the medical profile and I'll need the pro-con reports on Dawson, Downey and Santiago.

**JO.** I'll get them.

**KAFFEE.** Sam, you're gonna prepare Dawson. Razor-sharp order taker. Stepford Marine.

**SAM.** Okay.

**KAFFEE.** *(to* **JO***)* Work with Downey two hours a day. Get him to stop squinting when he talks, he looks shifty.

(**KAFFEE** *starts to head for the door.*)

All I've got at my place is Yoo-Hoo and Sugar Smacks, so bring whatever you want. And don't wear that perfume, it wrecks my concentration.

**JO.** Really?

**KAFFEE.** I was talking to Sam.

(**JO** *and* **SAM** *exit.* **KAFFEE***'s left alone.*)

*(pause)* So this is what a courtroom looks like.

*(blackout)*

**End of Act I**

# ACT II

*(Lights up on **JESSEP**'s office.)*

**TOM.** Commander Stone to see you, sir.

**JESSEP.** Thank you, Tom.

*(**STONE** enters.)*

Walter, any news?

**STONE.** Not yet, sir. We've still got a few more tests to run, and they'll take a while. Even at that, I'm not certain I'm gonna be able to make a determination.

**JESSEP.** I see.

**STONE.** Colonel, it would help us to know what happened.

**KENDRICK.** It was a code red, the men were shaving his head.

**STONE.** The boy didn't die of a haircut.

**KENDRICK.** He died because that's what the Lord saw fit.

**JESSEP.** Mary Mother of God, Jon, give the Lord a rest, will you please?!

**KENDRICK.** *(beat)* Yes sir.

**JESSEP.** *(pause)* You look like hell. You get some rest yourself.

**KENDRICK.** Yes sir.

*(**KENDRICK** exits.)*

**JESSEP.** Walter, I don't want to pin you down to anything. I know you've got more tests to run, let me ask you this: What are the possibilities at this point?

**STONE.** It could've been any number of things, Nathan. They used a gag, it could've gotten stuck in his throat, there could have been poison on the rag, he could've had the hell scared out of him and had a heart attack. Like I said, we may never be certain. Sometimes it's a judgement call.

**JESSEP.** A heart attack?

**STONE.** He has a medical history that suggests the possibility of a slight coronary disorder. Nathan, what the hell kind of reckless nonsense did Kendrick have those men –

**JESSEP.** Why wasn't the coronary disorder detected before?

**STONE.** I said the possibility of a –

**JESSEP.** That's not an answer.

**STONE.** *(beat)* The symptoms – Santiago's symptoms, were most likely pointing to a hundred far less debilitating conditions. There were no red flags.

**JESSEP.** Is that what you're gonna say to a board of inquiry?

**STONE.** *(beat)* I don't understand.

**JESSEP.** Doctor, you give these men a thorough examination every three months. And every three months you sent Santiago back on that wall with a clean bill of health, am I wrong?

**STONE.** *(beat)* The symptoms weren't nearly –

**JESSEP.** Walter, you tell me: What can happen to a doctor's career because of something like this? *(pause)* You know what I think happened? I don't think it was a code red. I think Dawson and Downey got it into their heads to kill Santiago. I think, like you said, I think there had to have been poison on the rag.

**STONE.** It's a possibility.

**JESSEP.** How long have we known each other?

**STONE.** Four years.

**JESSEP.** Close on to five now. One of the first things I did when I got this command was request your assignment to the hospital. And the first thing I'll do when I leave is tell the folks in the situation room I want Walter with the big stones coming with me. I put my trust in you, Walter. I put the lives of my Marines in your hands. That's why I think it had to be poison. Go back and run those tests. You're the doctor. You're the damn good doctor. Whatever you say, I'll live with it.

*(beat)*

There's gonna be an investigation into the cause of death. And I'll do whatever I can for you, Walter.

STONE. *(pause)* Thank you, sir.

JESSEP. You're dismissed.

(STONE *turns and exits.*)

JESSEP. *(calling)* Tom!

TOM. *(entering)* Sir.

JESSEP. Find me Captain Markinson.

*(Lights up on the brig.)*

(KAFFEE *enters.* DAWSON *comes to attention.*)

DAWSON. Sir, Lance Corporal Harold W. Dawson, sir.

KAFFEE. Harold, why do you do that? I'm representing you in a murder trial, do you honestly think I don't know who you are? I thought we were through with that shit the night I struck an enlisted man without cause or provocation, which I couldn't help but notice you didn't report to anybody.

(DAWSON *says nothing.*)

*(beat)* I wanted to come by and give you some words of...you know, give you encouragement.

(KAFFEE *takes a folded piece of paper from his pocket, unfolds it, and reads:)*

Sit up straight.

(KAFFEE *folds up the piece of paper and puts it back in his pocket.*)

Look, I know I'm talking to a brick wall, but there are two things I'd like you to consider before we start. The first is that Commander Galloway and Lt. Weinberg and I are doing everything we possibly can for you. And the second is that we're gonna get creamed.

*(beat)*

Now that's not very confidence inspiring, I know.

DAWSON. It's alright. *(pause)* I'm not the one who needs confidence. After all, it's not up to me anymore, is it? *(pause)* You have to accept the consequences too.

*(beat)*

Right?

**KAFFEE.** *(beat)* Yeah, but you see, they're not my consequences to accept.

**DAWSON.** That almost makes it a little bit worse, doesn't it,
sir?

**KAFFEE.** *(beat)* Harold, we're gonna lose. And we're gonna
lose huge.

*(beat)*

Sit up straight.

*(Lights up on courtroom.)*

*(The participants are milling into place.* **KAFFEE** *and*
**ROSS** *cross paths.)*

Last chance. I'll flip you for it.

**SERGEANT AT ARMS.** Ten-hut.

**ROSS.** Too late.

*(***KAFFEE** *and* **ROSS** *take their places as* **RANDOLPH**
*enters.)*

**SERGEANT AT ARMS.** All those having business with this
General Court-Martial, stand forward and you shall be
heard. Colonel Julius Alexander Randolph is presid-
ing. God save the United States of America.

**RANDOLPH.** Before the judge advocate calls his first witness, I want to get some language clear. That without
objection, the sworn statements of the defendants
have been read to the members and entered into the
court record.

**ROSS.** No objection, sir.

**KAFFEE.** No objection.

**RANDOLPH.** And that without objection, the sworn statements made by twentyone members of Rifle Security
Company have been read to the members and entered
into the court record.

**ROSS.** No objection. Sir.

**KAFFEE.** No objection.

**RANDOLPH.** Is the Government prepared to present its
case?

**ROSS.** We are, sir.

**JO.** Please the Court, before we begin, may I ask if all these M.P.'s are really necessary?

**RANDOLPH.** Are they making you nervous?

**JO.** No, sir, they're projecting the image that the defendants are dangerous and/or a flight risk.

**ROSS.** The Court might alert Commander Galloway to the fact that the defendants are on trial for murder.

**JO.** The defendants, who have not been found guilty of *any* crime, are in handcuffs, and I'm certain that if they were to break free and make their escape, the four armed guards at the door could apprehend them. In fact it would appear that every sailor at the Washington Navy yard who isn't in this courtroom is guarding this courtroom.

**ROSS.** Judge, the Provost Martial felt the defendants should be a security priority. The Provost Martial is in charge of security on this base. I was following his advice.

**JO.** The Provost Martial's gonna feel like an idiot if someone steals one of our ships during this trial.

(**RANDOLPH** *laughs.*)

**RANDOLPH.** Take your seat, Commander. I.A.

**JO.** Yes sir.

**ROSS.** Government calls Commander Stone.

**SERGEANT AT ARMS.** Call Commander Stone.

(**STONE** *enters and crosses to the witness chair.*)

**ROSS.** Dr. Stone, for the record would you state your full name, rank and current billet, please.

**STONE.** Commander Walter Stone. My billet is internal medicine specialist, Guantanamo Bay Naval Hospital.

**ROSS.** Have a seat. How long have you been attached to the hospital at GITMO?

**STONE.** From October 1 of last year, to the present.

**ROSS.** And on 7 July of this year, did you have occasion to treat Private First Class William Santiago?

STONE. I did.

ROSS. Would you describe that treatment.

STONE. PFC Santiago was brought into the Emergency Room on the morning of the seventh at zero-zero-ten. He was coughing up blood and suffering from a lack of oxygen. He lost consciousness at zerozero-thirty-five.

ROSS. And what were your observations upon examination?

STONE. The most obvious things were the rope marks around his wrists and that his head was partially shaved. X-rays and lab work revealed that his lungs were filled with fluid bilaterally due to profound acidosis. That is to say a build-up of acid in the lungs.

ROSS. What causes acid to build up in a person's lungs?

STONE. If the muscles and other cells of the body begin burning sugar instead of oxygen, lactic acid is produced.

ROSS. And from the moment the cells begin burning sugar to the moment that the lungs are filled with fluid, how long does that take?

STONE. Ordinarily, about an hour.

ROSS. Doctor, you say "ordinarily," was this an unusual case?

STONE. Yes.

ROSS. How so?

STONE. In Santiago's case, the chemical reaction took less than 15 minutes.

ROSS. Why was the reaction sped up in Santiago's case?

STONE. He had to have ingested a poison of some kind.

KAFFEE. Your honor, we object at this point. The witness can only speculate as to what caused the reaction.

ROSS. Commander Stone is an expert medical witness, in this courtroom his opinion isn't considered speculation.

KAFFEE. Commander Stone is an internist, not a criminologist, and the medical facts here are ultimately inconclusive.

**RANDOLPH.** A point which I'm confident you'll illustrate to the jury on your cross-examination, so I'm sure you won't mind if the doctor's opinion is admitted now.

**KAFFEE.** Not at all, sir. Objection withdrawn.

**ROSS.** Dr. Stone, did Willy Santiago die of poisoning?

**STONE.** Absolutely.

**ROSS.** Are you aware that the lab report and the coroners report showed no traces of poison?

**STONE.** Yes I am.

**ROSS.** Then how do you justify –

**STONE.** There are literally dozens of toxins which are virtually undetectable under certain circumstances. The nature of the acidosis is the compelling factor in this issue.

**ROSS.** Thank you, sir.

*(Lights up on* **KAFFEE***'s apartment.)*

*(***SAM** *is on a mock witness stand.)*

**KAFFEE.** Doctor, other than –

**JO.** Don't call him doctor.

**KAFFEE.** Right. Good. Commander, other than the rope marks was there any sign of external damage?

**SAM.** No.

**KAFFEE.** No scrapes?

**SAM.** No.

**KAFFEE.** No cuts?

**SAM.** No.

**KAFFEE.** Bruises? Broken bones? Fat lip?

**SAM.** No.

**KAFFEE.** Commander, was there *any* sign of violence?

**SAM.** *(beat)* You mean aside from the dead body?

**KAFFEE.** Fuck!! I walk into that every goddam time!

**ROSS.** Your witness.

*(Lights up on courtroom.)*

**KAFFEE.** Commander, my clients say they didn't use poison, so what I'd like to do is just ask you a few questions to see if there couldn't possibly be another explanation.

**STONE.** Lieutenant, there's no other explanation. A layman would have to –

**KAFFEE.** A layman? Pardon me, Commander, but you're talking to a man who got a C+ in bio-chem. Twice. Now if I understand correctly, the fact that this process took 15 minutes and not 60 minutes is what led to your conclusion that Private Santiago was poisoned.

**STONE.** Yes.

**KAFFEE.** 60 minutes is about average?

**STONE.** Yes.

**KAFFEE.** In some people it might be more, in some people it might be less.

**STONE.** A little bit more, a little bit less.

**KAFFEE.** Commander, is it possible for a person to have an affliction, some sort of condition, which would render that person less capable of withstanding the lactic acid?

*(**STONE** says nothing for a moment.)*

Commander, is it poss –

**STONE.** If a person had a cerebral disorder, it's possible that it would take less than an hour.

**KAFFEE.** How 'bout a coronary disorder? Or condition, I think it's called. A coronary condition?

**STONE.** Lieutenant, we're talking about an 18 year-old Marine in extraordinary physical shape.

**KAFFEE.** The Marine Corps requires them to maintain a certain standard of physical fitness, isn't that right?

**STONE.** Standards which are even higher for the Marines in R.S.C.

**KAFFEE.** In fact, you give them thorough physical examinations once every three months, right?

**STONE.** That's right.

**KAFFEE.** Doctor, is it possible for a young man to have a coronary condition, where the initial warning signals were so mild that they could escape a doctor during a routine medical exam?

**STONE.** *(beat)* You have to understand. In medicine, though we'd *like* to be exact about –

**KAFFEE.** Well, that's the beauty of being the lawyer for the defense. I don't have to worry about "exact," I just have to worry about "Is it possible"?

*(beat)*

Is it possible?

**STONE.** There would've been symptoms.

**KAFFEE.** What kind of symptoms?

**STONE.** There are a hundred different symptoms of –

**KAFFEE.** Chest pains?

**STONE.** Yes.

**KAFFEE.** Shortness of breath?

**STONE.** Certainly.

**KAFFEE.** Fatigue?

**STONE.** I suppose, if the heart wasn't always pumping blood to the brain at the correct –

*(**KAFFEE**'s gotten a document from his table.)*

**KAFFEE.** Doctor, is this your signature?

**STONE.** Yes it is.

**KAFFEE.** This is an order for Private Santiago to be put on temporary restricted duty. Would you read your hand written remarks at the bottom of the page, please, sir.

**STONE.** *(reading)* "Initial testing negative. Patient complains of chest pains, shortness of breath, and fatigue. Restricted from running distances over five miles for one week."

**KAFFEE.** Thank you. I have no more questions.

**ROSS.** "Initial testing negative." That's what it says here. What kinds of tests were these.

**STONE.** All manner of –

**ROSS.** Cardio-vascular tests?

**STONE.** Yes.

**ROSS.** Cardio-pulminary tests, physical strength, endurance, in fact, in all, how many separate cardio-tests were administered to Santiago?

**STONE.** Seventeen.

**ROSS.** And did any of those 17 tests indicate that there might be something wrong with his heart?

**STONE.** No.

**ROSS.** The medical equipment you have in the CCU of the Guantanamo Naval Hospital, would you describe it as modern or outdated.

**STONE.** It's very modern equipment.

**ROSS.** In fact it's the same equipment used in the CCU of the Bethesda Naval Hospital here in Maryland.

**STONE.** That's right.

**ROSS.** The same Bethesda Naval Hospital where the President of the United States goes for his medical check-ups.

**STONE.** Yes.

**ROSS.** Dr. Stone, you've held a license to practice medicine for 20 years, you are board certified in internal medicine, you are chief of internal medicine at a hospital which serves over seventhousand people. In your opinion, was Willy Santiago poisoned?

**JO.** *(standing)* Please the Court, we renew our objection to Commander Stone's testimony, and ask that it be stricken from the record. And we further ask that the court instruct the jury to lend no weight to this witness's testimony.

> *(**KAFFEE** and **SAM** are dying, but they're trying to keep their poker faces. **RANDOLPH**'s gonna try to be polite about this, but he thought he made himself clear before.)*

**RANDOLPH.** The objection's overruled, Commander.

**JO.** Your Honor, the defense strenuously objects and requests a conference in chambers so that his honor might have an opportunity to hear discussion before ruling on the objection.

**RANDOLPH.** The objection of the defense has been heard and overruled. The witness is an expert and the Court will hear his opinion.

**JO.** Exception.

**RANDOLPH.** Noted.

**ROSS.** Doctor, in your expert opinion, was Willy Santiago poisoned?

**STONE.** No question about it.

**ROSS.** Thank you, sir, I have no more questions.

**RANDOLPH.** Commander, you can step down.

>(**STONE** *stands and exits.*)

**ROSS.** Please the Court, while the government reserves its right to call rebuttal witnesses should the need arise, we rest our case.

**RANDOLPH.** We'll stand in recess until Monday morning, at which time the defense can call its first witness.

>(**RANDOLPH** *raps his gavel.*)

**SERGEANT AT ARMS.** Ten-hut.

>(*The courtroom begins clearing out.* **KAFFEE,** **JO,** *and* **SAM** *are packing up their things.*)

**SAM.** *(to* **JO***)* I strenuously object? Is that how it works? Objection. Overruled. No, no, no, no, I *strenuously* object. Oh, well, if you strenuously object, let me take a moment to reconsider.

**JO.** I got it on the record.

**SAM.** You also got it in the jury's head we're afraid of the doctor. You object once so they can hear you say he's not a criminologist, any more than that and it looks like the great cross we did was just a lot of fancy lawyer tricks. Which was just what Ross was hoping for. It's the difference between paper law and trial –

**KAFFEE.** Sam –

**SAM.** Christ, you even had the judge saying Stone was an expert!

**KAFFEE.** She made a mistake, let's not relive it.

*(There's an uncomfortable silence.)*

**SAM.** I'm sorry. I'm in a pissy mood.

*(beat)*

I'm gonna call my wife. I'll see you tonight.

*(**SAM** starts to leave.)*

**JO.** Why do you hate them so much?

*(**SAM** stops and turns around.)*

**SAM.** They beat up on a weakling. And that's all they did. The rest is just smoke filled coffee-house crap. They tortured and tormented a weaker kid. And it wasn't just that night, read the letters, it was eight months. And you know what? I'll bet it was his whole life. They beat him up, and they killed him. And why? Because he couldn't run very fast.

**JO.** Do you think the argument we're gonna make on Monday is legally sound?

**SAM.** I think the argument we're gonna make on Monday is morally reprehensible.

**JO.** Since when do lawyers get to decide what's morally reprehensible?

**SAM.** Since when do Marines get to decide which laws they're gonna obey?

**KAFFEE.** Alright, that's enough. Jo, he's busting his ass for these guys, he doesn't have to be friends with them. And Sam, the only Marines we're concerned with are Dawson and Downey. Now everybody take the night off.

**SAM.** Danny, I –

**KAFFEE.** I mean it. We've been working 18 hour days for two weeks. Spend the night with your family. Jo, do whatever it is you do when you're not here. We'll work in the morning.

**SAM.** Shouldn't we –

**KAFFEE.** No.

> *(beat)*

Take the night off.

**SAM.** *(beat)* I'll see you tomorrow.

**KAFFEE.** Hey, I thought we had a pretty good day. You gotta hand it to Ross, though, he's very good.

**SAM.** He asked seven questions on his re-direct and sent the jury to bed with the image that Walter Stone is the President's doctor. He put Stone in his pocket with seven questions. I think he's just warming up.

> *(SAM exits.)*

**KAFFEE.** That was depressing.

**JO.** How much damage did I cause?

**KAFFEE.** It doesn't matter.

**JO.** Are you saying it doesn't matter 'cause it's water under the bridge, or it doesn't matter 'cause I didn't cause that much damage.

**KAFFEE.** I'm saying it doesn't matter 'cause we'll never know and there's nothing we can do about it.

**JO.** Good. That's a good attitude.

**KAFFEE.** What made you become a lawyer for the Navy?

**JO.** They wouldn't let me fly the planes or drive the boats.

**KAFFEE.** You are like seven of the strangest women I have ever met.

**JO.** I know. I'm the girl guys like you hated in sixth grade.

**KAFFEE.** Jo, you're the girl guys like me tortured in sixth grade. I'll see you tomorrow. *(pause)* Why do you like them so much?

**JO.** At this moment there's probably no one in the world that Dawson dislikes more than you. And if someone fired a gun at you, he'd stand in front of the bullet without thinking twice.

**KAFFEE.** *(pause)* Don't worry about the doctor. This trial starts Monday.

*(Lights up on an* **ORDERLY** *as* **MARKINSON** *enters.)*

*(***MARKINSON***'s wearing civilian clothes and has press credentials on his breast pocket.)*

**ORDERLY.** Can I help you?

**MARKINSON.** God, I hope so. I've been getting the run around all morning. Gilbert Hamilton, *Baltimore Sun-Times.*

**ORDERLY.** Hey, good sports section.

**MARKINSON.** The best.

**ORDERLY.** What can I do for you?

**MARKINSON.** I'm doing a two part feature on air traffic at different bases around the world, but I'm focusing mostly on Naval Air Station, Guantanamo Bay, and Andrews Airforce Base.

**ORDERLY.** Sounds interesting.

**MARKINSON.** Do you keep on file a record of incoming and outgoing flights?

**ORDERLY.** Anything that isn't classified, sure. We have copies of all the daily Tower Chief's Logs.

**MARKINSON.** Is that right?

**ORDERLY.** Sure. They list incoming and outgoing flights, passenger manifests…we just have the copies, though. The originals stay at the base.

**MARKINSON.** No problem. I need copies of the Tower Chief's Logs for Andrews and Guantanamo for the evening of July 6th/morning of July 7th.

**ORDERLY.** Got it. The only thing is, I need to see a Fleet requisition form and a 7-10 signed by two officers over the rank of Lieutenant.

**MARKINSON.** Oh hell.

**ORDERLY.** I'm sorry, but I can't show the log books without a Fleet requisition form and a 7-10 signed by two officers over the rank of Lieutenant.

**MARKINSON.** I understand. Is the duty officer here?

**ORDERLY.** No sir, he's at a department meeting.

MARKINSON. Gee whiz, is there anyone else I can speak to?

ORDERLY. Not for another half hour. Everyone's at lunch. I'm the only one here.

(**MARKINSON** *pulls out a pistol and trains it at the* **ORDERLY**.)

MARKINSON. Then let's go get some log books.

(*blackout*)

(*In the darkness, we hear the Marines chanting.*)

MARINES. I WANNA BE A RECON RANGER
I WANNA BE A RECON RANGER
I WANNA LIVE A LIFE OF DANGER
I WANNA LIVE A LIFE OF DANGER
STAND TALL
DO IT AGAIN
SING IT LOUD
THREE FOUR
LEFT RIGHT
ONE TWO THREE FOUR
ONE TWO
STAND PROUD!

(*Lights up on courtroom.*)

(**RANDOLPH** *enters.*)

SERGEANT AT ARMS. Ten-hut.

(**RANDOLPH** *takes his place.*)

RANDOLPH. Lt. Kaffee, are you ready to call your first witness?

KAFFEE. Yes sir. Defense calls Corporal Howard.

(**HOWARD** *enters.*)

ROSS. Corporal Howard, have you been previously sworn?

HOWARD. Yes sir.

ROSS. Would you state your full name, rank, and current billet for the record, please.

**HOWARD.** Corporal Jeffrey Owen Howard, Marine Barracks Windward, Guantanamo Bay, Cuba.

**ROSS.** Thank you, corporal, you can have a seat.

(**HOWARD** *sits.*)

**KAFFEE.** Corporal, are you a little nervous?

**HOWARD.** No sir.

**KAFFEE.** Would you like a glass of water?

**HOWARD.** No sir, I'm fine, thank you.

**KAFFEE.** You sure?

**HOWARD.** Yes sir.

**KAFFEE.** Well if you want some water or you'd like to take a short break, you let us know.

**ROSS.** Judge, the witness has twice said he doesn't want any water, can we –

**RANDOLPH.** *(to KAFFEE)* Lieutenant...

**KAFFEE.** Yes sir. Corporal, you've been called as a witness in order to give the Court a better insight into the nature of the duty of the Marines in RSC Windward. You should feel free to use the map that's behind you.

**HOWARD.** Yes sir. It's very simple, really. The base is divided into two halves –

**KAFFEE.** Corporal?

**HOWARD.** Sir?

**KAFFEE.** You're gonna have to wait for me to ask you a question.

**HOWARD.** Yes sir. I'm sorry, sir.

**KAFFEE.** *(pause)* Would you describe the general layout of the base for us, please?

**HOWARD.** Yes sir. It's very simple, really. The base is divided into two halves, the divider being Guantanamo Bay. Each half of the base has its own rifle security company. On the left side is RSC Leeward, see, and on the right is Windward.

**KAFFEE.** What's the function of the Marines in RSC Windward?

**HOWARD.** To provide ground support in the event of an enemy engagement, and to provide day to day security on the fenceline.

**KAFFEE.** How much time do the Marines spend on watch?

**HOWARD.** We're on the fence for one week, then off for a week.

**KAFFEE.** And when you're on the fence, how long is each watch?

**HOWARD.** Six hours on, six hours off.

**KAFFEE.** Six hours on, six hours off, one week on, one week off, is that right?

**HOWARD.** Yes sir.

**KAFFEE.** Are the sentries armed?

**HOWARD.** Yes sir.

**KAFFEE.** With...?

**HOWARD.** Sir?

**KAFFEE.** What are the Marines armed with?

**HOWARD.** Sir?

**KAFFEE.** What are you armed with, corporal?

**HOWARD.** Weapons.

**KAFFEE.** A pea shooter, a pocket knife, a sling-shot...?

**HOWARD.** Oh no, sir. A peashooter...pocket knife...That was funny, sir.

**KAFFEE.** Permission to lead the witness?

**RANDOLPH.** By a leash, if necessary.

**KAFFEE.** You're armed with M-16 rifles and 60 rounds of ammunition, is that right?

**HOWARD.** Yes sir.

**KAFFEE.** Okay. *(pause)* Corporal, what's a Code Red?

**HOWARD.** Sir a Code Red is a disciplinary action brought against a Marine who's fallen out of line.

**KAFFEE.** Name some ways a Marine could fall out of line.

**HOWARD.** Being late for Platoon or Company meetings, keeping his barracks in disorder, letting his personal appearance become substandard, behaving in a manner unbecoming a Marine, falling back on a run...

**KAFFEE.** Have you ever received a Code Red?

**HOWARD.** Yes sir.

**KAFFEE.** Would you describe it.

**HOWARD.** I dropped my weapon during a field exercise one day. We were doing seven-man assault drills and I dropped my weapon. It's just that my palms were sweaty 'cause it was over a hundred degrees and my weapon just slipped, sir.

**KAFFEE.** And what happened?

**HOWARD.** That night in my barracks, the guys in my squad threw a blanket over me and took turns punching me in the arm for five minutes. Then they poured glue on my hands.

**KAFFEE.** Okay, –

**HOWARD.** It worked too, 'cause I ain't never dropped my weapon since.

**ROSS.** Object.

**KAFFEE.** We're gonna have to strike that, Corporal, but it was a nice try. What happened after they punched you and poured glue on your hands?

**HOWARD.** They took me to the Post 44 and bought me a beer.

**KAFFEE.** They gave you a Code Red, then they bought you a beer.

**HOWARD.** Yes sir.

**KAFFEE.** Corporal, were you acquainted with Private Santiago?

**HOWARD.** Yes sir.

**KAFFEE.** Did you come in contact with him every day?

**HOWARD.** Yes sir.

**KAFFEE.** You participated in drills together?

**HOWARD.** Yes sir.

**KAFFEE.** Your squads were on the fence together?

**HOWARD.** Yes sir.

**KAFFEE.** You shared a barracks hall?

**HOWARD.** Yes sir.

**KAFFEE.** Was Private Santiago ever late for platoon meetings?

**HOWARD.** Yes sir.

**KAFFEE.** Was his barracks ever in disorder?

**HOWARD.** Yes –

**KAFFEE.** Did he ever let his appearance become substandard?

**HOWARD.** Yes –

**KAFFEE.** Did he ever fall back on a run?

**HOWARD.** All the time, sir.

**KAFFEE.** Did he ever, in your estimation, behave in a manner unbecoming a Marine?

**HOWARD.** Absolutely, sir, yes.

**KAFFEE.** Did he ever, prior to the night of July 6th, receive a Code Red?

**HOWARD.** No sir.

**KAFFEE.** Never? You got a Code Red 'cause your palms were sweaty, why didn't Private Santiago, this burden and embarrassment to his unit, why didn't he ever get a Code Red?

**HOWARD.** Corporal Dawson wouldn't allow it, sir.

**KAFFEE.** Corporal Dawson wouldn't allow it.

**HOWARD.** Hal was – Corporal Dawson, was Santiago's squad leader. He wouldn't let anyone go near him, sir. The guys talked tough about Santiago, but when it came down to it, they wouldn't touch him. They were too afraid of Corporal Dawson, sir.

**ROSS.** Object. The witness is characterizing.

**KAFFEE.** I'll re-phrase. Corporal Howard, did you ever want to give Santiago a Code Red?

**HOWARD.** Yes sir.

**KAFFEE.** Why didn't you.

**HOWARD.** 'Cause Dawson'd kick my butt, sir.

**KAFFEE.** Good enough. Lt. Ross is gonna ask you some questions now.

*(**ROSS** waits until **KAFFEE** has taken his seat. He picks up a copy of a thick book and walks to the witness stand.)*

**ROSS.** Corporal, I hold here "The Marine Guide and General Information Handbook for New Recruits." Are you familiar with this book?

**HOWARD.** Yes sir.

**ROSS.** Have you read it?

**HOWARD.** Yes sir.

**ROSS.** Good.

*(hands him the book)*

Would you turn to the chapter that deals with Code Reds, please.

**HOWARD.** I'm sorry, sir?

**ROSS.** Just flip to the page in that book that discusses Code Reds.

**HOWARD.** Code Reds aren't in this book, sir.

**ROSS.** I see.

*(goes back to his table and gets another book)*

Let's turn then to the "Marine Infantry Handbook." Would you find us the section on Code Reds in this book and read it to us, please.

**HOWARD.** Sir, you see, Code Red is a Marine term that – we only use it down at GITMO, sir. I don't know if it actually –

**ROSS.** We're in luck, then.

*(**ROSS** gets another book.)*

"The Marine Corps Guide for Sentry Duty, NAVBASE Guantanamo Bay, Cuba." I assume we'll find the term Code Red and its definition in this book, and then we can move on, am I correct, Corporal?

**HOWARD.** No sir.

**ROSS.** No? Corporal Howard, I'm a Marine. Is there no book, no manual or pamphlet, no set of orders or regulations that let me know that, as a Marine, one of my duties is to perform Code Reds?

**HOWARD.** No sir. No books, sir.

**ROSS.** No further questions.

*(KAFFEE gets one of the books from ROSS's table.)*

**KAFFEE.** Corporal, would you turn to the page in this book that says where the Enlisted Men's Mess Hall is?

**HOWARD.** Lt. Kaffee, that's not in the book, sir.

**KAFFEE.** No? You mean to tell the Court that you've been stationed in GITMO for 13 months, and in all that time you've never had a meal?

**HOWARD.** No sir. Three squares a day.

**KAFFEE.** I'm confused. How did you know where the mess hall was if it's not in this book?

**HOWARD.** I guess I just followed the crowd at chow time, sir.

**KAFFEE.** No more questions.

**HOWARD.** Thank you, sir.

**RANDOLPH.** We'll take a five minute recess, don't anybody go too far.

*(RANDOLPH raps his gavel.)*

**SERGEANT AT ARMS.** Ten-hut.

*(RANDOLPH exits.)*

As you were.

*(ROSS walks up to KAFFEE.)*

**ROSS.** Can I talk to you alone for a minute?

*(ROSS and KAFFEE cross away from the defense table.)*

That was nice work. The re-direct on Howard.

**KAFFEE.** Thank you.

**ROSS.** I want this to end now. I don't want Kendrick to have to take the stand.

**KAFFEE.** Yeah, he's a real day at the beach, isn't he?

**ROSS.** I was up half the night with him. He's bright, articulate, nothing in the closet, and you're gonna make a meal out of him.

**KAFFEE.** What are you getting at, Jack?

**ROSS.** That's what I wanted to ask you. You're putting on an entertaining defense that's going nowhere. Everyone expects you to do whatever you have to, but you start looking like you're enjoying it and you're gonna find yourself practicing law on a weather ship off Bayonne, New Jersey.

**KAFFEE.** We've got two minutes to the Reverend Kendrick, what can I do for you?

**ROSS.** Don't put him on the stand. I have to protect these guys, I can't allow them to look like clowns. Stop now. Three years a piece.

**KAFFEE.** Four weeks ago we were talking about six months.

**ROSS.** Four weeks ago your clients pissed on six months. Four weeks ago your clients weren't a daily feature in the Washington Post, and neither were you. You can tap dance all you want, at the end of the day, all you've got is the testimony of two men accused of murder.

**KAFFEE.** Tell me about it.

(**KAFFEE** *starts away.*)

**ROSS.** You got bullied into this room. By everybody. By Dawson, by Galloway, shit, I practically dared you. You got bullied into this room even though not for one second have you believed you could win. You got bullied into this room by the memory of a lawyer who might have stood a chance.

**KAFFEE.** *(pause)* You're a lousy fuckin' softball player, Jack.

**SERGEANT AT ARMS.** Ten-hut.

**ROSS.** Your guys are going down and I can't stop it anymore.

**KAFFEE.** Defense calls Lt. Jonathan James Kendrick.

**SERGEANT AT ARMS.** Call Lt. Kendrick.

(**KENDRICK** *walks to the witness chair.*)

**ROSS.** Lieutenant, have you been previously sworn?

**KENDRICK.** Yes I have.

**ROSS.** Would you state for the record your full name, rank and current billet, please.

**KENDRICK.** Lt. Jonathan James Kendrick, Executive Officer, Rifle Security Company Windward, Marine Barracks Guantanamo Bay.

**ROSS.** Thank you, Lieutenant, you can have a seat.

*(KAFFEE stands.)*

**KAFFEE.** Lt. Kendrick, in your opinion, was Santiago a good Marine?

**KENDRICK.** I'd say he was about average.

**KAFFEE.** Lieutenant, you co-signed three proficiency and conduct reports on Santiago. On all three pro-con reports, you indicated a rating of below average.

**KENDRICK.** Yes, Private Santiago was below average. I didn't see the need in trampling on a man's grave.

**KAFFEE.** We appreciate that, but you're under oath now, and I think, unpleasant as it may be, we'd all just as soon hear the truth.

**KENDRICK.** I'm aware of my oath.

**KAFFEE.** Lieutenant, these are the last three pro-con reports you signed for Lance Corporal Dawson. On the first two, you gave him a rating of exceptional, but on this most recent report, dated June 9th of this year, he received a rating of Below Average. It's this last report I'd like to discuss for a moment.

**KENDRICK.** That's fine.

**KAFFEE.** Dawson's ranking after Infantry Training School was perfect. Records show that well over half his class has since made full corporal, while Dawson's remained a Lance Corporal. Was Dawson's promotion held up because of this last report?

**KENDRICK.** I'm sure it was.

**KAFFEE.** Do you recall why Dawson was given such a poor grade on this report?

**KENDRICK.** I'm sure I don't. I have many men in my charge, Lieutenant, I write many reports.

**KAFFEE.** Do you recall an incident involving a PFC Curtis Barnes, who'd been found stealing liquor from the officer's club?

**KENDRICK.** Yes.

**KAFFEE.** Did you report Private Barnes to the proper authorities?

**KENDRICK.** I have two books at my bedside, Lieutenant. The Marine Code of Conduct, and the Kings James Bible. The only proper authorities I'm aware of are my commanding officer, Colonel Nathan R. Jessep, and the Lord our God.

**KAFFEE.** Lt. Kendrick, at your request, I can have the record reflect your lack of acknowledgement of this court as a proper authority.

**ROSS.** Objection. Argumentative.

**RANDOLPH.** Sustained. *(to* **KAFFEE***)* Watch yourself, Counselor.

**KAFFEE.** Yes sir. *(to* **KENDRICK***)* Did you report Private Barnes to your superiors?

**KENDRICK.** I remember thinking very highly of Private Barnes, and not wanting to see his record tarnished by a formal charge.

**KAFFEE.** You preferred instead to handle it within the unit.

**KENDRICK.** Yes I did.

**KAFFEE.** Lt. Kendrick, do you know what a code red is?

**KENDRICK.** Yes I do.

**KAFFEE.** Have you ever ordered a code red?

**KENDRICK.** No, I have not.

**KAFFEE.** Lieutenant, did you order Corporal Dawson and two other men to make sure that Curtis Barnes receive no food or drink except water for a period of five days?

**KENDRICK.** That's a distortion of the truth. Private Barnes was placed on barracks restriction. He was given water and vitamin supplements, and I assure you that at no time was his health in danger.

**KAFFEE.** Would the Court care to remind the jury that Lt. Kendrick is *not* a medical expert, and doesn't have the first clue as to whether or not Curtis Barnes' health was in danger.

**RANDOLPH.** The members are cautioned.

**KAFFEE.** Lieutenant, wouldn't this form of discipline be considered a Code Red?

**KENDRICK.** *(beat)* Not necessarily.

**KAFFEE.** If I called the other 379 members of RSC to testify, would *they* say it was a Code Red?

**ROSS.** Please the Court, the witness can't possibly testify as to what 379 Marines would say. We object to this entire line of questioning as argumentative and irrelevant badgering of the witness.

**RANDOLPH.** Lieutenant Kaffee, I would remind you that you're now questioning a Marine officer with an impeccable service record.

**ROSS.** Thank you, Judge.

**RANDOLPH.** You're welcome. I'm overruling your objection.

**KAFFEE.** Your Honor, I'm withdrawing the question.

*(beat)*

Lieutenant, was Corporal Dawson given a rating of Below Average on this last report because you'd learned he'd been sneaking food to Curtis Barnes.

**ROSS.** Object.

**RANDOLPH.** Not so fast. *(to* **KENDRICK***)* Lieutenant?

**KENDRICK.** *(pause)* Corporal Dawson was found to be Below Average because he committed a crime.

**KAFFEE.** What crime did he commit?

*(beat)*

Lt. Kendrick?

*(beat)*

Dawson brought a hungry guy some food. What crime did he commit?

**KENDRICK.** He disobeyed an order.

**KAFFEE.** And because he did, because he exercised his own set of values, he was punished, is that right?

**KENDRICK.** Corporal Dawson disobeyed an order.

**KAFFEE.** Yeah, but it wasn't a real order, was it? He wasn't being asked to secure a hill, or radio for battalion aid. I mean, surely a Marine of Dawson's obvious skill and intelligence should be able to determine on his own which orders he's gonna follow, and which orders might be, say, illegal.

*(beat)*

Lt. Kendrick?

*(beat)*

Can he?

*(beat)*

Can Dawson determine on his own which orders he's gonna follow?

**KENDRICK.** No, he can not.

**KAFFEE.** A lesson he learned after the Curtis Barnes incident, am I right?

**KENDRICK.** I would think so.

**KAFFEE.** You know so, don't you, Lieutenant.

**ROSS.** Object!

**RANDOLPH.** Sustained.

**KAFFEE.** Lt. Kendrick, one final question: If you had ordered Dawson to give Santiago the Code Red, –

**ROSS.** – please the Court –

**KENDRICK.** I told these men not to touch Santiago –

**KAFFEE.** – is it reasonable to think he could've disobeyed you again?

**ROSS.** Lieutenant, don't answer that.

**KAFFEE.** You don't have to, I'm through.

**ROSS.** Lieutenant Kendrick, did you order the defendants to give Willy Santiago a Code Red?

(**KENDRICK** *is glaring at* **KAFFEE**...)

**ROSS.** Lt. Kendrick, did you –

**KENDRICK.** No I did not.

*(blackout)*

*(Lights come up on* **KAFFEE**'s *apt as* **SAM** *enters with a large envelope.)*

**SAM.** This was sitting outside your door. It's marked urgent and personal.

**KAFFEE.** What is it?

**SAM.** My x-ray vision is failing me today, open the damn thing.

**KAFFEE.** Hey Mr. Sunshine –

**JO.** Knock it off. Anyone want anything from the kitchen?

**KAFFEE.** Yoo-Hoo, please.

*(***KAFFEE*** begins opening the envelope and looking at the contents.)*

**JO.** Sam?

**SAM.** I'll take a Yoo-Hoo.

**JO.** You want a Yoo-Hoo?

**SAM.** *(pause)* Yeah.

**JO.** Okay.

**SAM.** *(pause)* I want a Yoo-Hoo, is that such a big deal? He asks for a Yoo-Hoo and it's like he's asking for the correct time. I ask for a Yoo- Hoo and the world is coming to an end.

**JO.** *(to* **KAFFEE***)* What's in the envelope.

*(But* **KAFFEE** *is just staring at what's in his hands.)*

Danny?

**KAFFEE.** It's from Markinson.

*(Lights up on* **MARKINSON** *in a pool of light.)*

**MARKINSON.** "To Lt. junior grade Daniel A. Kaffee, United States Naval Reserve, Judge Advocate General's Corps. Lt. Kaffee, I know the following to be true: Colonel Jessep had no intention of transferring Private Santiago off the base. The transfer order you secured was written the morning of your arrival, six days after Private Santiago's death. Jessep's claim that the 0600 was the first available transportation off the base is a lie.

There was a flight that left for Andrews Airforce Base seven hours earlier. I've enclosed the two Tower Chief's Logs. You'll notice that while Colonel Jessep has removed the departure entry from the Guantanamo log, the arrival entry is in the Andrews log. Lieutenant, please don't waste valuable time and resources trying to find me. Save these men. Captain Matthew Andrew Markinson, United States Marine Corps."

*(Lights up on* **KAFFEE***'s apt.)*

**KAFFEE.** Sonofabitch!!

**SAM.** I don't believe this.

**KAFFEE.** Sonofa*bitch*!!

**SAM.** I'll call D.O.D. and find out if they're missing anything.

*(***SAM*** exits.)*

**JO.** We're home. I've gotta go tell Louden.

**KAFFEE.** Forget about Downey. I need you to pull every string you can. FBI, CIA, let's hire our own guys if we have to. We need Markinson. We have to have him.

**JO.** Why? We've got the log books and the letter.

**KAFFEE.** The letter's typed and there's no signature. The log books are photocopies.

**JO.** *(pause)* They're not admissable.

*(***SAM*** enters.)*

**SAM.** A Navy orderly was held up at gunpoint by a man posing as a reporter from the *Baltimore Sun-Times*.

**JO.** I'll get the originals.

**KAFFEE.** Don't bother. Jessep knows about the robbery by now and he's fixed the original Andrews log. I'd bet money on it.

**JO.** We'll find Markinson, how hard can it be?

**KAFFEE.** The man walked into the Pentagon and stole government property at gunpoint, and we didn't know about it until he sent us a note.

**JO.** And Jessep can just fix log books?

**KAFFEE.** Is Downey ready for tomorrow?

**JO.** Yes.

**KAFFEE.** Is he solid?

**JO.** Absolutely.

**KAFFEE.** Do you think we can find Markinson?

**JO.** Yes.

**KAFFEE.** *(to* **SAM***)* Do you?

**SAM.** Yes.

**KAFFEE.** We don't have a discovery obligation. Keep this from Ross for 24 hours.

**SERGEANT AT ARMS.** Ten-hut.

*(Lights up on the courtroom.)*

**KAFFEE.** Defense calls PFC Louden Downey.

*(***DOWNEY*** walks to the witness chair.)*

**ROSS.** Private Downey, would you raise your right hand and place your left hand on this bible.

*(***DOWNEY*** does.)*

Do you swear that the testimony you will give in this general court-martial will be the truth, the whole truth, and nothing but the truth, so help you God?

**DOWNEY.** Yes sir.

**ROSS.** Please sit.

*(Lights come up on ***MARKINSON***.)*

*(He is in full dress uniform.)*

**MARKINSON.** "Dear Mr. and Mrs. Santiago. I was William's Company Commander. I knew your son vaguely, which is to say I knew his name. In a matter of time, the trial of the two men charged with your son's death will be concluded, and seven men and two women whom you've never met will try to offer you an explanation as to why William is dead. Most likely they will offer you many explanations. For my part, I've done what I can to bring the truth to light. I've done it, not in the uniform in which I served for 21 years, but in costumes and in shadows. I was a defender. And at this moment I'm being pursued by the Naval investigative service, the federal bureau of investigation, the central intelligence agency, and the military police. And I can't possibly do this anymore. Because the truth is this: Your son is dead for only one reason. I wasn't strong enough to stop it. Always, Captain Matthew Andrew Markinson, United States Marine Corps."

(**MARKINSON** *waits a moment before he pulls the pistol from its holster, points the gun into his mouth, and fires.*)

(*blackout*)

(*Lights up on courtroom.*)

(**DOWNEY** *is still on the stand.*)

**DOWNEY.** We were taken into custody by the military police officers and taken to the brig.

**KAFFEE.** Private, this is my last question for you. Why did you give Santiago a code red on the night of July 6th?

**DOWNEY.** The code red was ordered by the Executive Officer, Lt. Kendrick.

**KAFFEE.** Thank you very much. (*to* **ROSS**) Your witness.

(**ROSS** *gets up.*)

**ROSS.** Private, for the day of six July, the Switch log has you down at Post 39 until 1600, is that correct?

**DOWNEY.** I'm sure it is, sir, they keep that log pretty good.

**ROSS.** How far is it from post 39 to the Windward barracks?

**DOWNEY.** It's a ways, sir, it's a hike.

**ROSS.** About how far by jeep?

**DOWNEY.** About ten, fifteen minutes, sir.

**ROSS.** Have you ever had to walk it?

**DOWNEY.** Yes sir. That day. Friday. I was DDL. The Pick-up Private – sir, that's what we call the guy who drops us at our posts and picks us up...also 'cause he can get girls in New York City – the Pickup Private got a flat. Right at 39. He pulled up and blam!...A blow-out with no spare. The two of us had to double time it back to the barracks.

**ROSS.** And if it's 10 or 15 minutes by jeep, I'm guessing it must be a good hour by foot, am I close?

**DOWNEY.** Pick-up and I did it in 45 flat, sir.

**ROSS.** Not bad. And you say your assault on Santiago was the result of an order that Lt. Kendrick gave at a platoon meeting at 16:20 hours?

**DOWNEY.** *(beat)* Yes sir.

**ROSS.** But you just said that you didn't make it back to Windward barracks until 16:45.

**DOWNEY.** *(pause)* Sir?

**ROSS.** If you didn't make it back to your barracks until 16:45, then how could you be at a platoon meeting at 16:20.

**DOWNEY.** *(pause)* You see, sir, there was a flat tire.

**ROSS.** Private, did Lt. Kendrick ever tell you to give Santiago a code red?

**DOWNEY.** *(pause)* Me?

(**JO** *leaps to her feet.*)

**JO.** Please the court, I'd like to request a recess in order to confer with my client.

**ROSS.** Who told you to give Santiago the code red?

**DOWNEY.** Ma'am?

**JO.** Private Downey has rights!

**ROSS.** Private Downey has been read his rights, Commander.

**DOWNEY.** *(confused)* Ma'am?

**RANDOLPH.** The question will be repeated.

**ROSS.** Who told you to give Santiago a code red?

**JO.** Your honor –

**RANDOLPH.** Take your seat.

**DOWNEY.** Hal?

**ROSS.** Did Corporal Dawson tell you to do it?

> (**DOWNEY** *looks at* **DAWSON**.)

**ROSS.** Don't look at him, look at me.

**DOWNEY.** Sir?

**DAWSON.** Private.

> *(Everyone looks at* **DAWSON**…*)*

> Answer the Lieutenant's question.

> *(long pause)*

**DOWNEY.** Yes, Lieutenant. I was given an order by my squad leader, Lance Corporal Harold W. Dawson of the U.S. Marine Corps. And I followed it.

> *(blackout)*

**MARINES.** What're you gonna do when you get back?

> What're you gonna do when you get back?

> Take a shower and hit the rack?

> Take a shower and hit the rack?

> Oh no

> Not me

> Oh no

> Not us

> What're we gonna do when we get back?

> Polish up for a sneak attack.

> *(Lights up on* **KAFFEE**'s *apt.)*

> (**JO** *and* **SAM** *are sitting in silence.*)

**JO.** Where do you think he is?

> (**SAM** *doesn't know.*)

**JO.** *(cont.)* As far as Downey was concerned, it was an order from Kendrick. He never distinguished between –

*(KAFFEE enters.)*

Danny, I'm sorry.

*(KAFFEE seems to be in an incredibly normal mood.)*

**KAFFEE.** Don't worry about it.

**JO.** Sam and I were just talking about how all we really need to do is put some witnesses on the stand who can talk about implied orders. Or maybe we put Downey back on the stand and then go to Dawson.

**KAFFEE.** Maybe if we work at it we can get Dawson charged with kidnapping the Lindbergh baby.

**JO.** *(pause)* Are you drunk?

**KAFFEE.** *(beat)* Pretty much. Yeah.

**JO.** *(pause)* I'll make a pot of coffee. We've got a long night's work ahead.

**KAFFEE.** *(to SAM)* She's gonna make coffee. *(to JO)* He wasn't at the meeting.

*(amazed)* He – he wasn't even there.

*(beat)*

That was…that was an important piece of information, don't you think?

**JO.** *(pause)* It was just a setback. But we fix it. We fix it and we get to Markinson.

**KAFFEE.** Markinson's dead.

*(beat)*

He got into full dress uniform, drew a nickel plated revolver from his holster and fired a bullet into his mouth. He was at the Beltway Motor Lodge. It's three blocks from here.

*(beat)*

Anyway…since we seem to be out of witnesses, I thought I'd drink a little.

**JO.** I still think we can win.

**KAFFEE.** Then maybe you should drink a little.

**JO.** We go to Randolph. Right now. We get a 24 hour continuance.

**KAFFEE.** Why would we do that?

**JO.** To subpoena Colonel Jessep.

**KAFFEE.** *(pause)* What?

**JO.** Listen for a second –

**KAFFEE.** No.

**JO.** Just hear me out –

**KAFFEE.** No. I won't listen to you and I won't hear you out. Your passion is compelling, Jo. It's also useless. 'Cause Louden Downey needed a trial lawyer today.

**JO.** You walk away from this now, you have sealed their fate.

**KAFFEE.** Their fate was sealed the moment Santiago died.

**JO.** You have to call Jessep.

**KAFFEE.** I don't have to do shit.

**JO.** Why did you ask for the transfer order?

**KAFFEE.** *(beat)* What are you –

**JO.** In Cuba. Why did you ask for the transfer order. Why did you ask nicely.

**KAFFEE.** What does it matter why I –

**JO.** Why?!

**KAFFEE.** I wanted the damn transfer order!

**JO.** Bullshit! You could've gotten it by calling any one of a dozen departments at the Pentagon. You didn't want the transfer order. You wanted to see Jessep's reaction when you asked for it. You had an instinct, and it was confirmed by Markinson. Now dammit, let's put Jessep on the stand and end this thing.

**KAFFEE.** What possible good will come from putting Jessep on the stand?

**JO.** He told Kendrick to order the code red.

**KAFFEE.** He did? Why didn't you say so. I assume you've got proof. No, wait, I forgot, you were sick the day they taught law at law school.

**JO.** You put him on the stand and you get it from him!

**KAFFEE.** We get it from him. Yes. No problem. *(to* **SAM***)* Colonel, isn't it true that you ordered a code red, coerced the doctor, forged a transfer order and fixed a log book?

**SAM.** Look, we're all a little –

**KAFFEE.** I'm sorry, your time's up. What do we have for the losers, judge? Well, for the defendants, it's a lifetime at exotic Fort Levenworth, where every day is Valentine's Day for our handsome young Marines. And for Lt. Kaffee? That's right – It's – A Court-Martial! Yes, Johnny, after falsely accusing a highly decorated Marine officer of conspiracy and perjury, Lt. Kaffee will have a long and prosperous career teaching typewriter maintenance at the Rocco Columbo School for Women. Thank you for playing "Should We or Should-We-Not Follow the Advice of the Galacticly Stupid"!!

*(***KAFFEE*** picks up a carton of documents and throws it to the floor. There's dead silence. Maybe just the sound of* **KAFFEE** *breathing after this outburst…finally)*

**JO.** I'm sorry I lost you your set of steak knives.

**KAFFEE.** Get the fuck out.

*(***JO*** picks up her briefcase and walks out.)*

*(***KAFFEE*** walks offstage.* **SAM** *starts picking up the papers that have scattered to the floor.* **KAFFEE** *walks back in with a bottle of Jack Daniels.)*

Stop cleaning up.

*(But* **SAM** *continues.)*

Sam. Stop cleaning up.

*(***SAM*** stops. They both sit.)*

You want a drink?

**SAM.** *(beat)* No.

**KAFFEE.** *(pause)* Is your father proud of you?

**SAM.** Don't do this to yourself.

**KAFFEE.** Is he? Is he very proud of you?

**SAM.** *(pause)* Yes.

**KAFFEE.** I'll bet he is. I'll bet he bores the shit outa the neighbors. Guys he works with, aunts, uncles…" Sam made law review. Sam's got a big case he's making. He's – he's arguing, he's making an argument." *(pause)* I think my father would've enjoyed seeing me graduate from law school. I think he would've liked that. An awful lot.

*(beat)*

Did you know the man spent half his life defending the Constitution of the United States and the other half trying to prove he wasn't a Communist.

*(beat)*

And he died young. And he died tired.

*(beat)*

I'm very angry about that, Sam.

**SAM.** *(pause)* He'd have been proud of you yesterday. You should've seen yourself thunder away at Kendrick. It was a sight to see. He'd have been proud of you yesterday.

**KAFFEE.** What about today?

**SAM.** Today you did the best you could.

**KAFFEE.** *(pause)* We should go talk to Dawson.

**SAM.** I'm gonna miss being in charge of socks and underwear.

**KAFFEE.** *(pause)* What?

**SAM.** I was just making a dumb –

**KAFFEE.** Socks and underwear.

**SAM.** Yeah.

**KAFFEE.** In the file. Jo had the inventory of his footlocker.

**SAM.** What are you –

**KAFFEE.** Who knew that Santiago wasn't being transferred. Name the people.

**SAM.** Jessep –

**KAFFEE.** Right –

**SAM.** Kendrick –

**KAFFEE.** Who else?

**SAM.** Markinson.

**KAFFEE.** And Santiago.

**SAM.** What?

**KAFFEE.** Willy Santiago knew he wasn't being transferred off the base. Santiago knew. Why it took me five weeks to figure this out is beyond me, but given time, I'll think of a way to blame it on you. Let's go. I need you to prep me on Jessep and I need Jo to get the continuance.

**SAM.** What the hell are you talking about?

**KAFFEE.** I'll explain it in the car.

**SAM.** You still need a witness.

**KAFFEE.** I have a witness.

**SAM.** A dead witness.

**KAFFEE.** And in the hands of a lesser attorney, that'd be a problem. Let's go.

**SAM.** No. Wait a second –

**KAFFEE.** The cover-up isn't our case. To win, Jessep has to tell the jury that he ordered a code red.

**SAM.** And you think you can get him to just say it?

**KAFFEE.** I think he wants to say it. I think he's pissed off that he's gotta hide from us. I think he wants to say that he made a command decision and that's the end of it. He eats breakfast 80 yards away from 4000 Cubans who are trained to kill him, and no one's gonna tell him how to run his unit. Least of all the pushy broad, the smart Jew, and the Harvard mouth. If I can make him defend himself, if I can just make him defend himself, he'll say he ordered the code red. Let's go.

**SAM.** You'd need a window. He has no weaknesses, he won't let you near him.

**KAFFEE.** He has a weakness.

**SAM.** What?!

**KAFFEE.** He thinks he was right. Let's go.

(*blackout*)

(*Lights up on the dark courtroom.*)

(**JO** *is sitting by herself in the witness chair.*)

Say, Sam? Have you ever heard the story of Lt. Commander Galloway and Lt. Colonel Jessep?

**SAM.** I believe I have, Danny. It's a story of courage and conviction, is it not?

**KAFFEE.** Right you are. Commander Galloway was investigating a crime, and she had a question she wanted the Colonel to answer.

**SAM.** This Colonel is a very intimidating character, I've heard.

**KAFFEE.** Well, sure, to some people. To some people he's the stuff of which nightmares are made.

**SAM.** But not to Commander Galloway.

**KAFFEE.** No sir. 'cause Commander Galloway ain't scared a nothin'. She had a question. And she was gonna get an answer.

(*beat*)

And she was confident. And she was relentless…

(**KAFFEE** *drops the routine and speaks directly to* **JO**.)

…and she did her job.

**JO.** What do you want?

**KAFFEE.** I want to talk to you about Lance Corporal Dawson and PFC Donnelly.

**SAM.** Downey.

**KAFFEE.** Downey.

**JO.** I don't want to talk to you anymore.

**KAFFEE.** No, I can't accept that. We braved extraordinary elements to get over here. My car ran out of gas halfway up Eigth Street. Sam had to walk a quarter of a mile to get help. Anyway, the wife and I were thinkin' about maybe going into Court tomorrow and saving our clients' lives, maybe stickin' some homicidal maniacs behind bars to boot. We thought you might wanna come along. What do you say?

**JO.** *(pause)* I can't seem to defend people.

*(KAFFEE kneels down next to JO.)*

**KAFFEE.** I'm sorry you feel that way. You're my hero, Joanne. From the first day. You were a lawyer.

*(beat)*

Live with that.

**SERGEANT AT ARMS.** Ten-hut.

*(The trial participants begin filing in.)*

*(RANDOLPH wraps his gavel.)*

**RANDOLPH.** Lieutenant Kaffee, are you prepared to call your witness?

**KAFFEE.** Your Honor, I don't suppose it would do any good to make a motion for dismissal at this point.

**RANDOLPH.** I'm glad to see you still have your sense of humor, Lieutenant.

**KAFFEE.** Defense calls Colonel Nathan Jessep.

**SERGEANT AT ARMS.** Colonel Nathan Jessep is called.

*(JESSEP walks in and stands in front of the witness chair.)*

**ROSS.** Colonel, have you been previously sworn, sir?

**JESSEP.** I have not.

**ROSS.** Would you raise your right hand and place your left hand on the bible. Do you swear that the testimony you give today in this general court-marital will be the truth, the whole truth, and nothing but the truth, so help you God?

**JESSEP.** I do.

**ROSS.** Would you state your full name, rank, and current billet for the record please, sir.

**JESSEP.** Colonel Nathan Robert Jessep, Commanding Officer, Marine Ground Forces, Guantanamo Bay, Cuba.

**ROSS.** Would you have a seat please, sir?

(**JESSEP** *sits.*)

**KAFFEE.** Colonel, when you learned of Santiago's letter to the NIS, you had a meeting with your two senior officers, is that right?

**JESSEP.** Yes.

**KAFFEE.** The platoon Commander, Lt. Jonathan Kendrick, and the company Commander, Captain Matthew Markinson.

**JESSEP.** Yes.

**KAFFEE.** And at present, Captain Markinson is dead, is that right?

**ROSS.** Objection, I'd like to know just what defense counsel is implying.

**KAFFEE.** I'm implying simply, that at present, Captain Markinson is not alive.

**ROSS.** Surely Colonel Jessep doesn't need to appear in this courtroom to confirm that information.

**KAFFEE.** I just wasn't sure if the witness was aware that two days ago, Captain Markinson took his own life with a .45 calibre pistol.

**RANDOLPH.** The witness is aware, the Court is aware, and now the jury is aware. We thank you for bringing this to our attention. Move on, Lieutenant.

**KAFFEE.** Yes sir. *(to* **JESSEP***)* Colonel, at the time of this meeting, you gave Lt. Kendrick an order, is that right?

**JESSEP.** I told Kendrick to tell his men that Santiago wasn't to be touched.

**KAFFEE.** And did you give an order to Captain Markinson as well?

**JESSEP.** I ordered Markinson to have Santiago transferred off the base immediately.

**KAFFEE.** Why?

**JESSEP.** I felt that his life might be in danger once word of the letter got out.

**KAFFEE.** Grave danger?

**JESSEP.** Is there another kind?

*(**KAFFEE** holds up a document.)*

**KAFFEE.** We have the transfer order that you and Markinson co-signed, ordering that Santiago be lifted on a flight leaving Guantanamo at six the next morning. Was this the first flight off the base?

**JESSEP.** The 0600 was the first flight off the base.

**KAFFEE.** Colonel, you flew up to Washington early this morning, is that right?

**JESSEP.** Yes.

**KAFFEE.** I notice you're wearing your class A dress uniform for your appearance in Court today.

**JESSEP.** As are you, Lieutenant.

**KAFFEE.** Did you wear that uniform on the plane?

**ROSS.** Please the Court, is this dialogue relevant to anything in particular?

**KAFFEE.** The defense didn't have the opportunity to depose this witness, your honor, we'd ask the Court for a little latitude.

**RANDOLPH.** A very little latitude.

**KAFFEE.** Colonel?

**JESSEP.** I wore fatigues on the plane.

**KAFFEE.** And you brought your dress uniform with you.

**JESSEP.** Yes.

**KAFFEE.** A toothbrush? A shaving kit? Change of underwear?

**ROSS.** Your honor –

**KAFFEE.** *(to **ROSS**)* Is the Colonel's underwear a matter of national security?

**RANDOLPH.** *(to **KAFFEE**)* Get somewhere fast with this, Lieutenant.

**KAFFEE.** Yes sir. Colonel?

**JESSEP.** I brought a change of clothes and some personal items.

**KAFFEE.** Thank you.

> (**KAFFEE** *gets a document from his table.*)

After Dawson and Downey's arrest on the night of the sixth, Santiago's barracks room was sealed and its contents inventoried.

*(reading)* "4 pairs of camouflage pants, 3 long sleeve khaki shirts, 3 short sleeve khaki shirts, 3 pairs of boots, 4 pairs of green socks, 4 pairs of black socks, 3 olive-green tee-shirts, 2 belts, 1 sweater – "

**ROSS.** Your honor, is there a question anywhere in our future?

**RANDOLPH.** Lt. Kaffee, I have to –

**KAFFEE.** I'm wondering why Santiago wasn't packed.

> (*That landed.*)

This is a telephone record of all calls made from your base in the past 24 hours. After being subpoenaed to Washington, you made three calls. I've highlighted those calls in yellow. Do you recognize those numbers?

**JESSEP.** *(looking over the printout)* I called Colonel Fitzhughes in Quantico, Virginia, to let him know I'd be in town. The second call was to Congressman Richmond of the House Armed Services Committee, and the third call was to my sister Elizabeth.

**KAFFEE.** Why did you make that call, sir?

**JESSEP.** I thought she might like to have dinner tonight.

**ROSS.** Your honor –

**RANDOLPH.** I'm gonna put a stop to this now.

> (**JO**'s handed **KAFFEE** another printout and a stack of letters.)

**KAFFEE.** Your honor, these are the telephone records from GITMO for July 6th. And these are 14 letters that Santiago wrote in nine months requesting, in fact begging, for a transfer off the base. *(to **JESSEP**)* Upon hearing the news that he was finally being transferred, Santiago was so excited, that do you know how many people he called? Zero. Nobody. Not one call to his parents saying he was finally getting out. Not one call to a friend saying can you pick me up at the airport. He was asleep in his bed at midnight, and according to you he was getting on a plane in six hours, and everything he owned was folded neatly in a footlocker and hanging neatly in a closet. You were leaving for one day and you packed a bag and made three phone calls. Santiago was leaving for the rest of his life, and he hadn't packed a thing, and he hadn't called a soul. Can you explain that? *(pause)* The fact is, Santiago wasn't going anywhere, isn't that right, Colonel?

**ROSS.** Object. Your Honor, it's obvious that Lt. Kaffee's intention this morning is to smear a high ranking Marine officer in the desperate hope that the mere appearance of impropriety will win him points with the jury. It's my recommendation, sir, that Lt. Kaffee be reprimanded for his conduct, and that the witness be excused with the Court's deepest apologies.

**RANDOLPH.** *(pause)* Overruled.

**ROSS.** Your Honor –

**RANDOLPH.** The objection's noted.

**KAFFEE.** *(beat)* Colonel?

(**JESSEP**'s smiling…and now he can't help but laugh.)

**KAFFEE.** Is this funny, sir?

**JESSEP.** No. It's not. It's tragic.

**KAFFEE.** Do you have an answer?

**JESSEP.** Absolutely. My answer is that I don't have the first damn clue. Maybe he was an early riser and he liked to pack in the morning. And maybe he didn't have any friends. I'm an educated man, but I'm afraid I can't speak intelligently about the travel habits of William Santiago. What I do know is that he was set to leave the base at 0600. Now are those really the questions I was called here to answer? Phone calls and footlockers? Please tell me you've got something more, Lieutenant. Two Marines are on trial for their lives. Please tell me their lawyer hasn't pinned their hopes to a phone bill.

*(beat)*

**JESSEP.** Do you have any other questions for me, Counselor?

*(The room is silenced. Jessep's slammed the door.)*

*(**KAFFEE** looks around the room, sees that the world is waiting for him to do something.)*

**RANDOLPH.** Lt. Kaffee?

*(**KAFFEE** says nothing.)*

Lieutenant, do you have anything further for this witness?

*(**KAFFEE** doesn't respond. **JESSEP** gets up to leave.)*

**JESSEP.** Thanks Danny. I love Washington.

**KAFFEE.** Excuse me, I didn't dismiss you.

*(**JESSEP** turns around.)*

**JESSEP.** I beg your pardon?

**KAFFEE.** I'm not through with my examination. I didn't dismiss you. Siddown.

**JESSEP.** Colonel.

**KAFFEE.** What's that?

**JESSEP.** *(to **RANDOLPH**)* I want the man to address me as Colonel or Sir. I believe I've earned it.

**RANDOLPH.** Defense counsel will address the witness as Colonel or Sir.

**JESSEP.** *(to **RANDOLPH**)* I don't know what the hell kind of an outfit you're running here.

**RANDOLPH.** And the witness will address this Court as Judge or Your Honor. I'm quite *certain* I've earned it. Take your seat, Colonel.

*(**JESSEP** goes back to the stand.)*

**JESSEP.** What would you like to discuss now? My favorite color?

**KAFFEE.** Colonel, the six a.m. flight, it was the first one off the base?

**JESSEP.** Yes.

**KAFFEE.** There wasn't a flight that left seven hours earlier and landed at Andrews Airforce Base at 2 a.m.?

**RANDOLPH.** Lieutenant, I thought we covered this.

**KAFFEE.** Your Honor, in just a moment defense will be calling Airman Cecil O'Malley and Airman Anthony Perez to the stand. Airmen O'Malley and Perez were working the ground crew on the morning of the seventh.

**ROSS.** Your Honor, these men weren't on the list.

**JO.** Rebuttal witnesses, Your Honor, called specifically to refute testimony offered under direct examination.

**RANDOLPH.** I'll allow the witnesses.

**KAFFEE.** Colonel, a moment ago –

**JESSEP.** Check the Tower Logs, for Christ's sake.

**KAFFEE.** We'll get to the airmen in just a minute, sir. A moment ago you said that you ordered Kendrick to tell his men not to touch Santiago.

**JESSEP.** That's right.

**KAFFEE.** And Kendrick was clear on what you wanted?

**JESSEP.** Crystal.

**KAFFEE.** Any chance Kendrick ignored the order?

**JESSEP.** Ignored the order?

**KAFFEE.** Any chance he just forgot about it?

**JESSEP.** No.

**KAFFEE.** Any chance Kendrick left your office and said, "The ol' man's wrong?"

**JESSEP.** No.

**KAFFEE.** When Kendrick spoke to the platoon and told them not to touch Santiago, any chance they ignored him?

**JESSEP.** Have you ever served in an infantry unit, son?

**KAFFEE.** No, sir.

**JESSEP.** Ever served in a forward area?

**KAFFEE.** No sir.

**JESSEP.** Ever put your life in another man's hands, ask him to put his life in yours?

**KAFFEE.** No sir.

**JESSEP.** We follow orders, son. We follow orders or people die. It's that simple. Are we clear?

**KAFFEE.** Yes sir.

**JESSEP.** Are we clear?

**KAFFEE.** *(beat)* Crystal.

*(pause)*

Colonel, I have just one more question before I call Airman O'Malley: If you gave an order that Santiago wasn't to be touched, then why would it be necessary to transfer him off the base?

*(And **JESSEP** has no answer. Nothing. He sits there, and for the first time, seems to be lost.)*

**JESSEP.** I'm sorry, would you repeat that?

**KAFFEE.** If you gave an order for Santiago not to be touched, then why would it be necessary –

**JESSEP.** Private Santiago was being transferred because he was a substandard –

**KAFFEE.** But that's not what you said. You said he was being transferred because he was in grave danger.

**JESSEP.** *(pause)* Yes. That's correct, but –

**KAFFEE.** You said, "He was in danger." I said, "Grave danger?" You said –

**JESSEP.** Yes, I recall what –

**KAFFEE.** I can have the Court Reporter read back your –

**JESSEP.** I know what I said. I don't need it read back to me like I'm a damn –

**KAFFEE.** Then why the two orders?

*(beat)*

Colonel?

*(beat)*

Why did you –

**JESSEP.** Sometimes men take matters into their own hands.

**KAFFEE.** No sir. You made it clear just a moment ago that your men never take matters into their own hands.

Your men follow orders or people die. So Santiago shouldn't have been in any danger at all, should he have, Colonel? *(pause)* It's a paradox, isn't it? Paradox is a word that means –

**JESSEP.** You little bastard.

**ROSS.** Your honor, I'd like to ask for a recess to –

**KAFFEE.** I'd like an answer to the question, Judge.

**RANDOLPH.** That makes two of us.

**KAFFEE.** If Kendrick told his men that Santiago wasn't to be touched, then why did he have to be transferred?

*(beat)*

Colonel?

*(beat)*

Kendrick ordered a code red, didn't he? Because that's what you told Kendrick to do.

**ROSS.** Object!

**RANDOLPH.** Counsel, you're putting words in –

*(***KAFFEE*** will plow through the objections of* **ROSS** *and the admonishments of* **RANDOLPH***.)*

**KAFFEE.** And when it went bad, you cut these guys loose.

**ROSS.** Your Honor –

**RANDOLPH.** Counsel, I'll hold you in contempt.

**KAFFEE.** You had Markinson sign a phony transfer order –

**ROSS.** Your Honor –

**KAFFEE.** You coerced the doctor –

**RANDOLPH.** This is your last warning!

**KAFFEE.** You doctored the log books.

**ROSS.** Dammit Kaffee!!

**RANDOLPH.** Consider yourself in contempt.

**KAFFEE.** I'll ask for the fourth time: If you ordered –

**JESSEP.** You want answers?!

**KAFFEE.** I'm entitled to them.

**JESSEP.** You want answers!!??

**KAFFEE.** I want the truth!!

**JESSEP.** You can't handle the truth!

(*beat*)

'Cause the truth is that we live in a world that has walls, and those walls need to be guarded by men with guns. Who's gonna do it? You? You, Lt. Weinberg? I have a greater responsibility than you can possibly fathom. You weep for Santiago and you curse the Marines. You have that luxury. The luxury of the blind. The luxury of not knowing what I know: that Santiago's death, while tragic, probably saved lives. And my existence, while grotesque and incomprehensible to you, saves lives. You can't handle it. 'Cause deep down in places you don't talk about at parties, you want me on that wall. You need me on that wall.

(*beat*)

We use words like honor, code, loyalty...We use these words as the backbone to a life spent defending something. You use them as a punchline. I have neither the time nor the inclination to explain myself to a man who rises and sleeps under the blanket of the very freedom I provide, then questions the manner in which I provide it. I'd prefer you just said thank you and went on your way. Otherwise, I'd suggest you pick up a weapon and stand a post. Either way, I don't give a damn what you think you're entitled to.

**KAFFEE.** (*quietly*) You ordered the code red.

**JESSEP.** (*beat*) I did the job you sent me to do.

**KAFFEE.** You ordered the code red.

**JESSEP.** You're goddam right I did.

(*There's a stunned pause...*)

**KAFFEE.** Please – Please the Court, I suggest the members be dismissed so that we can move to an immediate Article 39A session. The witness has rights.

(*beat – not unsympathetically*)

Jack.

**ROSS.** I concur.

**RANDOLPH.** The Sergeant at Arms will take the members to an ante-room where you'll wait until further instructions.

**JESSEP.** What the hell's going on? Captain? What the hell's going on? I'm not familiar with Article 39A. I did my job. I'd do it again. Now I'm getting on a plane and going back to my base.

**RANDOLPH.** Guard the prisoner.

**JESSEP.** What?!

**ROSS.** M.P.'s, guard the prisoner.

**JESSEP.** I ordered a code red and everybody's going to pieces like a fuckin' ladies auxiliary.

**ROSS.** Colonel Jessep, you have the right to remain silent. Any statement you do make can be used against you in a trial by Court-Martial or other judicial or administrative proceeding. You have the right to consult with a lawyer prior to questioning. This lawyer may be a civilian lawyer retained at no cost to the United States, or by a military lawyer appointed to act as your counsel.

**JESSEP.** *(over the reading of the rights)* I'm being charged with a crime? I'm – that's what this is – What – this is funny, you know that, this is –

(**JESSEP** *makes a quick move toward* **KAFFEE***, but he's grabbed by the* **M.P.***'s.*)

I'm gonna tear your eyes right outa your head and piss in your dead skull! You fucked with the wrong Marine!!

**ROSS.** Colonel Jessep, do you understand these rights as I've just read them to you?

(**JESSEP** *stares at* **ROSS** *– then looks around the courtroom.*)

**JESSEP.** You fuckin' people. You have no idea how to defend a nation. All you did was weaken a country tonight, Kaffee. That's all you did, give yourself a pat on the back. You put people in danger tonight. Sweet dreams, son.

**KAFFEE.** Don't call me son. I'm a lawyer and an officer of the United States Navy. And you're under arrest you sonofabitch. *(to the* **M.P.** *'s)* The witness is excused.

*(blackout)*

*(We hear the* **MARINES** *chanting…)*

**MARINES.** Lift your head and lift it high…

*Lift your head and lift it high…*

Corporal Dawson's passin' by…

*Corporal Dawson's passin' by…*

Left Right…

*Sound Off…*

Sing it loud…

*Do it again…*

*Three Four*

*Sound Off*

*Right Left*

*Stand Proud!*

*(The lights come up on the courtroom.)*

*(***RANDOLPH** *is staring at a piece of paper.)*

**RANDOLPH.** On the charge of Murder in the Second Degree, the Members find the defendants Not Guilty.

*(beat)*

On the charge of Conspiracy to Commit Murder, the Members find the defendants Not Guilty.

*(beat)*

On the charge of Conduct Unbecoming a United States Marine…the Members find the defendants Guilty as Charged.

*(For a moment, a little energy drains out of the room… but then things move ahead as if it were the simplest of formalities.)*

The defendants are hereby sentenced by this Court to time served in the brig up until this point, and are ordered to be Dishonorably Discharged from the Marine Corps.

*(He takes a moment.)*

**RANDOLPH.** This Court-Martial is adjourned.

**SERGEANT AT ARMS.** Ten-Hut.

*(***RANDOLPH*** leaves the room. Everyone moves very slowly or not at all. They gather up papers and pack up briefcases in silence. **DAWSON** and **DOWNEY** don't seem sure what to do now. An **M.P.** takes their handcuffs off.)*

**DAWSON.** No.

**KAFFEE.** Harold, I'm sorry.

**DOWNEY.** I don't understand.

**JO.** It's not as bad as it seems.

**DOWNEY.** Colonel Jessep said he ordered the Code Red.

**JO.** I know, but –

**DOWNEY.** Colonel Jessep said he ordered the Code Red. What'd we do wrong?

**KAFFEE.** Listen –

**DOWNEY.** What'd we do wrong?

**SAM.** Ask Dawson.

**DAWSON.** We did nothing wrong.

**SAM.** A jury just said your conduct was unbecoming a Marine. What does that mean?

**DAWSON.** You're the lawyer.

**SAM.** You're the Marine.

**DAWSON.** Not anymore.

**DOWNEY.** Hal, I don't understand.

**DAWSON.** *(to* **DOWNEY***)* Look –

**DOWNEY.** What does it mean?

**DAWSON.** It means we beat the shit out of the wrong guy.

**DOWNEY.** I'm serious. What did that mean?

**DAWSON.** You're gonna have to stop asking that.

**SERGEANT AT ARMS.** Kaffee, I gotta take these guys down to personnel for some paperwork.

*(***KAFFEE*** nods to the **SERGEANT AT ARMS***, who begins to take the defendants off.)*

**KAFFEE.** Harold!

**DAWSON.** Sir!

**KAFFEE.** You don't need to wear a patch on your arm to have honor.

*(pause)*

**DAWSON.** Ten-hut.

*(beat)*

There's an officer on deck.

(**DAWSON** *and* **DOWNEY** *snap and hold a salute to* **KAFFEE**. *After a moment, he returns the salute.*)

Sir. Permission to be dismissed.

**KAFFEE.** *(beat)* You're dismissed.

(**ROSS** *walks up to* **KAFFEE**.)

**ROSS.** Airmen Cecil O'Malley and Anthony Perez? What are they, second base and shortstop for the Toledo Mud Hens?

**KAFFEE.** I wouldn't lie to the court, Jack. O'Malley and Perez worked the ground crew at Andrews the morning of the seventh.

**ROSS.** And they saw the plane land?

**KAFFEE.** I never said that.

**ROSS.** *(smiles)* Good job.

**KAFFEE.** The people had a case, Jack.

*(They shake hands.)*

**ROSS.** I'll see you around the campus. I've gotta go arrest Kendrick.

**KAFFEE.** Tell him I say hi.

(**ROSS** *exits.*)

**JO.** How 'bout a celebration. I'm buying. Sam?

**SAM.** Maybe later. I'm gonna go home and talk to my daughter. I think she's gotta be bilingual by now.

(**SAM** *exits.*)

**JO.** So what's next for you?

**KAFFEE.** Staff Sergeant Hector Baines. He went to the movies on company time. What about you?

**JO.** Me? Oh, you know, the usual.

**KAFFEE.** Just annoying people?

**JO.** Yeah. *(pause)* So how 'bout it? You wanna have a drink?

**KAFFEE.** I'll hook up with you later. I'm gonna get started on Hector Baines. Stand my post for a while.

**JO.** *(pause)* You are like seven of the strangest men I have ever met.

*(She exits.)*

*(**KAFFEE** closes up his briefcase and starts to walk out.)*

**KAFFEE.** Lift your head and lift it high… Daniel Kaffee's passin' by…

*(blackout)*

# OTHER TITLES AVAILABLE FROM SAMUEL FRENCH

## THE FARNSWORTH INVENTION

### Aaron Sorkin

*Drama / 15m, 3f*

It's 1929. Two ambitious visionaries race against each other to invent a device called "television." Separated by two thousand miles, each knows that if he stops working, even for a moment, the other will gain the edge. Who will unlock the key to the greatest innovation of the 20th century: the ruthless media mogul, or the self-taught Idaho farm boy?

The answer comes to compelling life in *The Farnsworth Invention*, the new play from Aaron Sorkin, creator of *The West Wing* and *The Social Network*.

"Vintage Sorkin and crackling prime-time theater...breezy and shrewd, smart-alecky and idealistic."
– *Newsday*

"A firecracker of a play in a fittingly snap, crackle and pop production under the direction of Des McAnuff, the drama has among its many virtues the ability to make you think at the same time that it breaks your heart."
– *Chicago Sun-Times*

"The most exciting new play on Broadway...a rousing theatrical experience."
– *MTV News*

SAMUELFRENCH.COM

# OTHER TITLES AVAILABLE FROM SAMUEL FRENCH

## MEN OF TORTUGA

### Jason Wells

*Drama / 5m*

Four men conspire to defeat a despised opponent by a ruthless act of violence: they will fire a missile into a crowded conference room on the day of an important meeting. Maxwell, a hero of the old guard, volunteers to sacrifice himself for the plan. Then Maxwell meets Fletcher, an idealist with a "Compromise Proposal" designed to resolve all conflicts. Maxwell regards the Compromise as hopeless, but he develops a liking for Fletcher - a distressing fact when Maxwell learns that, if the conspiracy proceeds, young Fletcher will be among the dead.

As the scheme spins wildly into complication, the plotters descend into suspicion, bloodlust and raucous infighting, while Fletcher is drawn, inexorably, into the lion's den.

"Calling all corporate conspiracy theorists: Jason Wells has written a play confirming everything you've ever wanted to believe about what goes on behind the frosted windows and code-locked doors of America's executive suites…ripping, blacker-than-black satire… Wells' work, though almost blank in details, carefully exposes the barbarism encoded in corporate bureaucracy. With a grand sense of humor about misinterpreted metaphors and think-tank buzz language – 'he eats our bread' refers to someone you can trust – *Tortuga* gives us absurd savages in suits, drinking good bourbon and plotting destruction… Eat their bread."
– *Time Out Chicago*

10567846

CPSIA information can be obtained
at www.ICGtesting.com
Printed in the USA
LVOW13s2237130617
538026LV00008B/448/P